———————◆———————

I pulled the note out and read it. It was penciled almost
laboriously onto white-rag notebook paper, as if the
writer wanted to shout each word:

William is missing.
Cyril Weber. He knows about the Taurus connec-
tion. I know about you, Mr. Ace. You will help me.
See me at 201 Walnut Street, Newport Beach.

Mary Jarn

If I stayed out of it, that dead, curled-up, pale body
would stick in my brain forever.

I pulled out of the lot. Traffic was still light. It was
quiet. I knew Mary Jarn would have died uselessly unless
I fulfilled her wishes. And I needed to know why she had
chosen me. Her "presence" was already draped around
my soul.

———————◆———————

BLOODY
SILKS

Merle Horwitz

KNIGHTSBRIDGE PUBLISHING COMPANY
NEW YORK

Published in the United States by
Knightsbridge Publishing Company
255 East 49th Street
New York, New York 10017

ISBN: 1-877961-02-7

10 9 8 7 6 5 4 3 2 1
First Edition

To win,
place,
and show
bettors everywhere

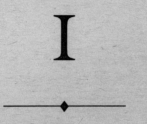

1

———◆———

She was standing next to me before it happened. In the midst of the crescendo of the crowd I had the sensation of instant urgency unrelated to the game I was playing. There was always a sense of urgency at a racetrack. People rush to judgment urgently, gulp their foot-long dogs urgently and down their beers urgently, stand in lines shifting from foot to foot and heel to toe urgently, breathe urgently. A sense of shattering significance surrounds the field and the grandstands, and pinches the valves leading to each heart.

The girl tugged at my jacket for the second time—urgently. Then she collapsed.

I don't know how they always find me. People in trouble. But they do. I work at keeping to myself. But still, wherever I go, strangers grab my sleeve and want me to locate their wayward daughter, find their son, or uncle, or rich aunt; sometimes their real father or mother. My past sticks with me like alimony.

It was late June and the sun was having trouble clearing away the overcast. Suddenly this sallow-faced girl with a size-too-large dark winter dress and matching wide eyes appeared at the table and pulled my binoculars from my nose. "Mr. Ace?" Her arms were thin and her skin was almost translucent.

I pulled away. She grabbed my sleeve like they all do

and insisted, "Harvey Ace? . . . I know it's you. Please. . . ." She held out a piece of paper. Before I could reply or move away or do anything else, she did it for me.

The race started. I heard the starting bell delayed by distance from the gate. The crowd roar struck the air around me. June's melancholy sky descended down into the Turf Club and around my throat. I held my breath while the girl's eyes rolled up into her lids and she caved in and slithered to the floor. The horses glided into the first turn, and here, at my feet, a wide-eyed young woman had all at once stopped living. She was white as the slip of paper in my hand. Her mouth was slightly open. She was curled into an angry U-shape. As she slumped to the ground, her left cheek slid along the smudged glazed floor. Stained alabaster against the dirt. A bubble gum wrapper stuck to her black hair. I stuffed the note into my pocket and reached down, automatically, to help her as if my touch might create life. She was cold.

There was hoarse screaming all around that was not about life or death. It was about horses that were racing and people who were playing games.

◆

"She couldn't have been more than twenty-four, Harvey," Doc Pinner said to me. His pudgy hands always moved when he talked. Now they were trembling. He was accustomed to occasional drunks, broken hips, bruised piles, aches and pains of overstrained jockeys, but not unexplained deaths quietly reached—eyes open, full of fear. His round face was distant and hurt. "You know," he sighed, "a racetrack is a shitty place to die. It ought to be illegal."

"Go tell it to the mountain."

"What was she doing with you?" he inquired a little suspiciously, one eyebrow raising in a sharp arch.

"She wasn't with me, Doc. I'm telling you. I don't know what she wanted." His lips puckered. He didn't believe me. My reputation, I thought. Somehow, all the innocence I could stuff into my grey-blue eyes was not enough to diminish one's natural suspicion of tailor-made clothing and Countess Mara ties. "Doc, I'm retired, you know that," I sighed. "I stay away from trouble—especially dying people. I've had my fill of that." The wide, stricken, horrified black eyes of the girl the moment death grabbed her were glued into my mind's eye. It reminded me of the fearful silence of children suffering.

"I'd like to know why she died, Ellis. There's not a mark on her. She just exhaled and died at my feet and kept staring." I shivered involuntarily. "By the way, can't we get out of this miserable place?" We had been in the morgue. In fifty-four years and unforgotten encounters with the dying and the dead I still couldn't think of the dead as actually gone. The existence of a form, a body, was the same as the existence of a presence for me and it always brought me down and stayed with me for a while, particularly at night.

"You're right." He lifted his knee and pressed it against the drawer, which slid shut. "I forget how cold it gets in here. It freezes your mind." As the hollow sound of the reverberating drawer faded, Ellis Pinner touched my shoulder and I turned. "You look like the doctor, Harvey. You're so goddamn crisp. Look at your nails—cleaner than mine." He put his manicured hand on top of mine. He was right.

We walked out of the chilling room into grey warmth and into four blue security uniforms.

"Always in the middle, aren't you Ace?" Sammy Rosenstock said, looking like he had cornered Attila the Hun. His flat boxer's nose aimed upward at my chin as if inviting a hook. He had been known as a counter-puncher in his glory days. A curling grey fringe of wiry hair contrasted with my straight thin cut, flattened back from my slightly receding forehead.

"The chief of Track Security is always in the middle, Sam. Not me."

"Well, you knew her, didn't you? A half-dozen eyeballs put you there."

"I don't care what they say. I'm not involved, don't know her, don't want to. It's your problem, Sam my boy. All yours. Not mine."

Sam spread his feet, right foot slightly forward. He carried his right foot in a bucket, as they say. Not good for a boxer. He could take a punch that way, absorb the force, but he couldn't move. "She was seen giving you something. That's what they say. That's exactly what they say." Sam Rosenstock's black eyes squinted. He was about to raise his left forefinger and point it at me, but I touched the back of his palm and held it firmly in place. The chief had studied my history thoroughly, drew back and settled for dropping his hand onto his hip. He and I had tangled before and he had lost. Counterpunchers can't win if they're over fifty and kept their right foot in a bucket. "That's so, isn't it?" he insisted. I knew he wouldn't dare to search me.

"No, Sam. It's not so. I don't know anything about this . . . whatever it is. I don't take cases anymore. You know that. I'm trying to change my destiny. *You* find out what killed her. Do your job and leave me be. . . ." I cracked a grin. "You're okay, Sam, but if you haven't anything else to say I've got a race to catch." I turned. Doc Pinner was smiling. "See you, Doc," I said and waved, turned, and headed for the men's room to wash my hands which was a quirk of my personality.

My table was at the finish line, four rows up into the

lap of the Turf Club. It was just before the sixth race. My race for the week.

That's the way it'd been. Watching racing animals for a clue and poring over racing charts, hiding from the world. It was the best medicine I could take at this point in my life. I had stopped looking for lost people. Too many years searching for me while in search of others. That's what it was all about, you know. People like myself and my former commander, Llewelyn Mackin, avoid the truth about ourselves in the quest for the truth about those who disappear.

2

◆

The sun came out. Spreads of green grass in the infield wandering between blue pools, spraying fountains, graceful swirls of white stock and orange and red pansies always gave me a sense of peace on earth midst the tremors before a race. This time my sense was one of vague fear and I looked around the tables to see who the eyewitnesses might have been. I could see the distant faces clearly, sharply. But as I surveyed the faces closer to me I felt the urge to put my glasses on and clean up the fuzziness. They were specially crafted. They folded into a pocket-watch-size compact. My arms were still long enough to avoid using them except during rare moments.

When I did, I thought of my father—sandy hair that never seemed grey dusting his forehead, sitting on a shoe dog's stool, adjusting his spectacles in an elaborate ceremonial way, as he stuck his nose into high-heeled pumps and announced the price to a breathless matron as if she had just won a trip to Miami. I resisted the urge. Seeing clearly the hair growing out of Mrs. Teaford's ear as she sat at her table below me did not ease my anxieties.

I remembered what I would be doing if I were still a finder. My mind would thumb through my card index and each name would trigger memory calls and I would struggle to recall the stored details. I kept a five-by-seven card file on every human being I met or heard about since

I began working for Army Intelligence. No one who had any relationship to any case in which I was involved escaped that insatiable file. Addresses; spouses' names; doctors, dentists, lovers and suspected lovers were indexed; physical ailments, drinking habits; colleges, high schools; parents' and siblings' names and addresses were all there. By this winter of '87 it had become encyclopedic. If I had had enough courage, I would have buried it at sea and forgotten all the aches of the past, but I kept it all and was afraid to lose my memories.

Finally, I forced myself to pay attention to business.

The amateurs wearing San Marino suede and Beverly Hills cutesy knit finery rushed to the $2 windows. Husbands and afternoon lovers shaded their eyes to catch a glimpse of the tote board, as if they were seriously thinking of betting a long shot. I knew the Turf Club dilettantes stuck with Pincay and Shoe as jockeys, and Hawley—if he was in from the East. And they stuck with Whittingham and Frankel as trainers. You seldom got a price when those nice people were involved with a horse. Once in a while Shoemaker got a price because he kept old loyalties and rode for trainers or owners who weren't always in the top ten. But the Wednesday-afternoon doctors who were sometimes there on Thursday and Friday, too, were sure to stay within the 5-to-1 range.

The sixth race is reserved for allowance fillies and mares, and you get a class animal now and then. I looked over the crowd and saw Tony Antonnini. I motioned and he came over. I gave him ten hundred-dollar bills. He knew what to do. He went directly to the large transaction window. I had the horse that was going to win. All the other races were playtime. My choice was one of the two "closers" in a sprint in which the speed for the first quarter was like 21.2 and between 44 and 45 for the half. It was too fast for this group to sustain. One of the closers needed more track. The other had a trainer who was bright and intuitive about his business.

The odds on my horse dropped from 12 to 1, to 10 to 1, and I knew that at the next flash she would be down to 8. I used my long stride to reach the betting area quickly and nodded to Tony, and he stepped in front of the window again and very slowly began to bet #5—Spin It. If he took his time and played his delay game long enough, and I did the same, we might keep the odds at 8 or 9 to 1. We wanted to keep the smart board watchers away. I put my long, angular frame in front of the window next to Tony.

I had the nauseous sensation that someone I had to fear was measuring the back of my neck. Either someone was sending out electric kill signals directed at me or my old private eye self was just doing tricks with my nervous system.

"Hi, Fred," I smiled at the counter man. "How's the gang? Sue and the kids?"

" 'Lo, Harv. You just get here? Got one going today?"

I just stood there and smiled at him and gazed down at the program lazily and then back up at him again.

He fidgeted. "Well, what will it be, Harv?"

"I think maybe I want #3 but I might settle for #5. What do you think, Fred?"

"Harvey Ace, you never asked anybody's advice—about the horses at least—and you know it. Now who do you want?"

It was getting closer to post time.

I turned to Joe. "Hi, Tone. Say, what are you buying?"

The announcer told the crowd that the horses were at the gate.

"Well, Harvey," he said, thoughtfully, "I'm buying either #3 or #6. You?"

"I like #3 too, Tone."

Fred said in an unfunny rasp. "Let's get with it, Harv. Cut it out."

"Give me two win tickets on #5, Fred."

He punched them out with this ink-smudged, wide thumb.

"Give me four more of the same."

The man behind me started to shove. "Move it, buddy," he said.

I stood my ground. "Four more of the same, Fred, nice and easy so they come out smiling."

He did and at the same time handed a $10 bill to an open counter man and held his hand up and spread out all five fingers.

There was only one minute left. Tony Antonnini and I walked away and stared at the tote board. He gave me all of his tickets and I stuffed one back into his hand. "Thanks, Tone."

"I'd like to see you when you get time for me." I thought I detected something flat in his voice.

I nodded. I had been handing him "extra" tickets for years. We had come to that worried ground between alien borders where a mutually created boundary substituted for an otherwise unacceptable tension. We were close but there was ground between us. During the years we had drifted into these lines and they seemed comfortable to both of us.

Horse Blanket Billy sat at my table. He didn't look up. We could sit for hours sometimes and not speak a word.

When the next flash came up, #5 was 9 to 1. There would be one more change on the board. I looked back at Fred. Sure enough, his hand kept going up with all five fingers.

I shoved the tickets into my shirt pocket. Then I reached into my jacket and fingered the slip of paper the girl had given me. I wasn't going to read it. At least not until after the race. I wouldn't be able to deny my instincts

forever. I would have to read it, and I would have to
react. That's the way it was. Also, I wanted to read it in
privacy away from all the eyes and decided to wait until
I entered my only domain of complete solitude, my XJ6
with the extra-dark tinted windows, sunroof, and jazzed-
up engine. It was my sweetheart. Insulated. Quiet.

I raised the binoculars.

The flag was up. The gate flipped open. Only after the
animals had leaped forward did the sound of the starter's
bell touch my ears. Number 5 got a clean if unspectacular
start.

When the horses came around into the stretch, Spin
It was laying fourth. The first two furlongs went in 21.3.
Very fast for this bunch. Too fast. When I saw the time
on the board I was convinced that we would catch them,
but the filly was still seven or eight lengths out of it on
the far turn. No matter how sure a gambler is, he is never
sure. The three speedsters were still clawing for the lead.
My brain told me they had to stop soon and crawl the
rest of the way home. Horse Blanket Billy began to
scream and wave his arms. Then Spin It got into gear
and it was all over.

3

I love to count money. There's a spiritual fascination about winning and then slowly, lovingly, counting the loot. It must be part of the fun of robbing banks. You get involved in the spiritual process of winning and touching the immediate results of the victory. I've often thought that winning by a knockout, or winning a horse race, were the only exulting victories left that were not totally destructive. I was aware of my own almost desperate need to win. There was nothing wrong with losing, I told myself, and told myself, and told myself.

I pulled the note out and read it. It was penciled almost laboriously onto white-rag notebook paper, as if the writer wanted to shout each word:

William is missing.
Cyril Weber. He knows about the Taurus connection. I know about you, Mr. Ace. You will help me. See me at 201 Walnut Street, Newport Beach.

Mary Jarn

If I stayed out of it, that dead, curled-up, pale body would stick in my brain forever.

I pulled out of the lot. Traffic was still light. It was quiet. I knew Mary Jarn would have died uselessly unless

I fulfilled her wishes. And I needed to know why she had chosen me. Her "presence" was already draped around my soul.

◆

From Parker Center I turned right and stepped briskly northward. October's Indian summers would soon turn downtown L.A. into a white incandescence. Although City Hall towered over me, it was now a rather dwarfish clean cement building just east of the modern oblongs stacked on Bunker Hill, the new city.

I could picture Llewelyn Mackin's black hair curled against a perspiring forehead as he waited, always as if on the edge of a monumental discovery. We had thirty years of connections between us. When he wasn't in his cubicle on the sixth floor of police headquarters, hunched over a phone, chewing the eraser end of an Eberhard, acting out his role of senior detective, Metro Squad, he was sitting near Olvera Street, in the shaded plaza, watching the pigeons and the fountain, waiting—strewing popcorn about, causing pigeon fights and grunting to himself deep in his inner being.

"You look contented," I said, rousing him from preoccupation.

"Um . . . guess I'm feeling like that."

"Not sure I believe you. But it's okay."

His brows arched and he wiped the perspiration from his forehead. "It's a quiet day, Harvey. Don't make problems . . . if you please."

"I won't. I promise. But I have to tell you something—and find out something."

"That's always been trouble," he sniffed, his meaty finger up to my nose. I smelled a slight trace of scotch on his breath rising as if from a smoldering mountain. "You were untrustworthy at the age of four. . . ." The finger crawled back into his pocket.

"And a snoop at the age of seven——."

"A gambler at twelve."

"A lover at sixteen . . . or was it fifteen?" I couldn't remember.

"A miserable sonofabitch hunting down forgotten war criminals, at twenty-three—and——."

"And—?"

"I'm running out. . . ."

The big detective sighed slowly. "I guess you're right." Silence. "Something sure as hell drove us to this kind of life, Harvey. Something."

The afternoon shifted. A trifling breeze touched us.

He spread a handful of popcorn around the edge of the fountain and laughed as the pigeons beat their feathers to get it. "Julia must have something to do with it. This getting-ready-to-retire business . . . waiting for the good life."

"It's hard to put you in the retired category, Lew. You're never up here unless your mind is going a mile a minute. Something's going on other than a quiet walk in the park."

"Harvey—" he pulled at his chin. "Why don't you just go away? This is *my* plaza. I didn't invite you. I don't see you for two or three months then suddenly you're on my fuckin' case. Get your own damn plaza and pigeons. I'm on the city payroll now and I can't be bothered with former private eyes."

I pulled back. "The city pays for dead time at Olvera Street but you haven't got five minutes for auld lang syne? Some friend." I sat next to him, on a dusty green bench. "Piss on you."

"Cut it out. I'm just trying to move through these last weeks on the force easily. It's Julia's influence. You know . . . for maybe the first time, I feel contented when she's around. Everything slows down. I'm retiring—money in the bank—a little bit, anyway. Too little. Just imagine—travel—."

"You've seen it all."

"Adventure," he laughed.

"You've had it all," I answered.

"Love."

"That's always new."

I shook my head. Passersby gesticulated in large Latin exaggerations. Mexican jukebox melodies drifted on warm blue air from the open door of a tourist restaurant.

A bus stopped. Its brakes suffered through a long groan. Giggling grammar school children unloaded and danced in jittery circles while teachers pointed and shushed and scolded. Soon tourists would fill the plaza and the sense of summer quiet would rush away.

"What'll you do when you retire, Lew?"

"Nothing special. Just want to leave with a good record. No statistical leftovers. Then surround myself in luxury, like you. With my pension and maybe a job with Sam at the track . . ." There was a question in his voice.

"Not convincing."

The pupils of his eyes were nearly as wide as the irises. They were like deep brown agates. "So it doesn't fit. Look, let's get to the point. Tell me why you're here. Your call wasn't helpful. In fact, I shouldn't even talk to you. I never get a call unless you're in trouble."

He was right.

"I am in trouble," I said. "I'm in the middle of a murder and I don't know why. Somehow my life fits someone else's ideas. Anyway, I'm in the middle. I need to know about a certain Mary Jarn."

I told him most of the story. Habit kept me from telling about the note.

"Something's wrong," he said. "Either you're holding

out or something's wrong and you're worse off than you think."

I didn't answer. Waited.

"I think you ought to forget the whole thing. Just stay away from it. The case will get to my desk eventually. The glorious LAPD detective squad will see to society's needs. You're retired. Remember?"

I nodded. "I got the picture. I complain and I get the finger, I don't complain and I get killed. I think your coming retirement has gotten the best of you."

"Just tell me what you've left out."

I felt myself smile. Can't hide anything from Llewelyn. Two-ton thinking machine.

"All I know is that Mary Jarn put me in the middle, and it's got my skin tingling. You know the feeling. I need information."

<hr>

Back at headquarters, Llewelyn dialed 81. I always made mental notes of internal station numbers.

"— get that homicide file from Holly Park, the duplicate. Thanks . . . now." He swiveled toward me, face flushed, fatter and older than when he was my superior in the army.

The file dropped onto his desk.

"Mary Jarn," he intoned. "Older brother, Henry Selmon. Mary was taken care of by Henry when their father died. Mother a drunk. Customary American horror story: Henry married Sylvia Rhinderman. They had the high life. Henry a well-known local jockey and suspected dope dealer. Quit riding and trained horses for Sarafin Stables. Walter Sarafin. Turkish immigrant, 1958. Big-time operator. Sylvia left Henry—Another American custom— and married wheeler-dealer Walter Sarafin. But . . ." he pulled at his jaw, his mind chewing up the facts.

". . . I know. Henry kept training for Walter."

"I suppose it figures if you throw enough money into the question."

"But from where?"

"From Turkey, from Mexico. From Tony Antonnini."

"You mean *Tony*? *My* Tony? With the sandpaper voice?"

"That's the one. It came from hash, cocaine . . . all of it. We can't convict or arrest but several years ago, with Antonnini as the point man, they made a killing. Big money. And we can't find it. I've been looking for it. . . ." He stopped and smiled.

"You're not in vice, Lew. That's not your bailiwick."

"Well, I've just been—so to speak—their expert: consultation. You and I didn't spend all those years in Europe for nothing, did we?"

It didn't feel right.

"You're in here, too, Harvey. Few nice words about your reputation and—"

Mackin looked up. I saw that same quizzical, furry-browed, eyes-narrowed look I remembered from the old days—a hundred years ago.

"She was talking to you before she died. And the note here says to question you about it."

I took a quiet, deep breath. The puzzle made no sense. At least my involvement in it didn't. But it seemed clean and neat. Gambler—private detective—mixed up with gamblers in dope transactions. Big ones. "It's much too neat, Lew. Someone *needs* me involved. I know all the players. Not Sylvia and Walter, but about them. Somebody has an ax to grind—on me."

"There's more. Mary Jarn was reported missing twice before, once by Tony Antonnini's son, William, a college boy. Henry didn't report it; William did. *He* reported *you* as a suspect. Wonder why he did that?"

"Good question. No answer. What about Henry . . .

read that to me . . . Here, just let me see that file . . ." I
reached for it.

Mackin jerked away. "Cut it out. Dammit. You're dealing with a fucking police file, Ace. You'll hear what I
choose for you to hear. Dammit, Harvey. You never
learn. Just sit there. There's nothing in the file that helps."

I stared. The outburst was not characteristic of Llewelyn Mackin. Thirty years ago I thought of him as the
perfect male machine—just a little heavy.

"Forget it, Harv. I'm touchy. Just want out of this. I
have visions of getting shot by some punk on the street
on the last day of my service, and it makes me crazy.
Something went wrong. You know? What happened? All
the years—."

Pain crossed back and forth over his face.

"Retire. Now," I suggested urgently. "Get out of here.
Marry Julia and get away. It's the system. The system
doesn't work for us . . . never did."

He pulled at his jowls. "I hate you when you're right.
You sonofabitch."

"You look miserable and unhealthy. Just coast . . . let
it all go. Hear?"

"If I could, I would. I swear. If I could, I would."

We rested. He disappeared in thought.

Finally he said, "Look. I'm gonna tell you something
important now. Like when I told you to go back to your
wife. To get her back no matter what. Remember, asshole?—That was important. So is this. . . ." His forefinger rested on the table, not pointing. Emphasizing. I
could tell there was a strange conflict in what he was
going to say. "Leave it all alone," he said. "Stay away
from this case. Don't let paranoia make you think anyone's out to get you."

I put my finger on his. "I don't believe it. I just plain
don't believe you." I started to rise. "Tell me one last
thing. Who is or was Cyril Weber?" I was more interested

in reaction than information. My own files might tell me all I needed. Or the phone book.

"Enough. There's nothing more here. Now get your ass out. I've done what I can. I'll call you the day I retire. You'll come to my wedding."

There was much more. And it was not in Llewelyn's file.

4

———◆———

I lived in a house I had owned for more than a decade. It shoved itself against a strip of beach next to the Marina del Rey channel. I got the house and Margaret got Kimberly, and I would have traded anytime. Margaret was less than an ideal homemaker, but she was an untiring playmate for my daughter. When we parted, I gathered up all the cash I could get hold of and gave it to her, and she and Kim returned to Rhode Island where her parents lived. She became famous as a magazine publisher. I had the house refurnished on the time plan and took to solitude as a way of life. But that's in the past and I try now to avoid reminiscing.

The beach was a good furlong to the water's edge and was generally lightly used. Just to the north, Venice and Santa Monica got all the traffic. All the hamburger stands and dinner and breakfast houses were up around Washington and Venice boulevards. And all the kids and all the noise. And all the street people, acrobats, jugglers, horn players, and near-naked sophomores, and all the hot dogs and popsicles and sidewalk vendors. And all the fun and most of the tragedy. The need to have quiet is as strong in me as the need to have companionship, and I bounce off ends of the poles with enough suddenness that I sometimes confuse myself.

The front door was open and I tensed up. I shoved it

wide and waited. Long honey-brown hair caressed the arm on my Sloans-on-sale leather couch.

"How'd you get in?"

She turned as if rolling on silk. "I managed."

"I want to know how you got in," my voice was insistent. I had dead-bolt locks on all the doors, and the sliding glass doors—upstairs and down—had floor locks and broom handles fitted to prevent them from sliding. I kept substantial amounts of cash in the house; it was my place of utter safety. "You have about one minute to tell me how you got in. I don't like anyone to surprise me like this, Elizabeth." I started counting by twos, staying at the door. When I got to 30 I moved toward her.

The teasing smile dropped from her lips and she said, "I had a key made. I made it. See. Here?" She held it up. "There's nothing to get mad at." She shook her head, petulantly reminding me of her age and the generation between us.

"Like hell there isn't. No one gets in this house without an explicit invitation. No one."

"What's explicit?"

"Give me the key and check Webster's. Or else stop pretending stupidity. I hate it."

Her hair cascaded in thick ringlets around olive-oil cheeks.

"Oh, all right. Here's your damn key. I thought it would be a nice surprise for you. See over there? Your dinner is all made. All I have to do is warm the scallopini and mushroom sauce, and all *you* have to do is squeeze lemon on it and stuff your face."

The candles were lit, too. I let go, and all my face and stomach muscles went sadly limp. Weary. It was 9 p.m. My whole body had been tied up in knots. Mary Jarn was still with me, in a tired, getting older body that didn't want interference in its more than half-century of accumulated routines.

"I haven't known you long enough to know if you've ever been more exhausted than you seem now. I'm sorry about the joke with the key," she explained.

She was one of the most alluring women I had ever met. Sex appeal erupted from her pores, yet she was oddly restrained in bed, just sufficiently lost in love making to make you believe that her mind had finally turned off and her body had turned on. But not by much. It was a strange, grey thin line. It made me suspect what she did with her time alone. Someone would come along and change the boundary lines one day.

"Just tell me—Miss Hume or Ms. Hume, whichever you prefer—how you did it. It's important or I wouldn't be so insistent." I tossed my jacket at her and sank into a deep, velour-covered easy chair, one I had found on Melrose near La Cienega and had had reupholstered.

Elizabeth took off my shoes and said, "Last Monday, in the afternoon, you fell asleep and I went shopping for dinner, and took your key and made an extra. It was simple. No mystery. You're always looking for the hard answers instead of the easy ones."

"Lizzie, dear. You can't do that sort of thing. You are old enough to understand and young enough to spook. Your marriages failed because you do not understand a man's psyche."

"That's not true," she said, hotly. "My first was to a drunk and second to a mean psycho—."

"What's that make me? Never mind. Just remember I live a private life. *Private*. I have to *let* you into it. You can't push your way in. It won't work . . . believe me, I know." I started to fumble with my shirt and she took over. I closed my eyes and breathed deeply.

"You are the loneliest man I ever met, Harvey Ace. And the hardest and the softest. You are an absolute challenge for a girl on the make." She sighed and laid her head in my lap.

So far as I knew she had grown up in South Pasadena and had been a Rose Princess the year she got married. She was twenty. Her husband was cut from his college football team and was drunk more than sober. She never mentioned his name. You could tell, she said, that his good looks would degenerate into an early bloated impotency. I thought she had an instinct for picking bums as lovers. It gave me pause.

I squirmed. "C'mon. I need to put my money away."

"You won?"

"Yes, I won." I hesitated and said, "And lost, too. And a young lady name Mary lost, too. And I don't know why or how, and I shouldn't really care. That much I know. I shouldn't care."

"But you do."

Through and through. I was sure I was through with caring. But this alabaster piece of flesh stopped living right at my feet and I cared. And worse, I gambled on a horse and told myself, "Cut it out, you don't care." It was obscene.

Pushing myself out of the encompassing ease of the chair, I began to pace, leopard-like, and I kept pushing it further away. "Where were you today? Besides here."

Her blue eyes darted away. She put my jacket over her arm. "I'll throw the shirt in the hamper."

I nodded. I decided to put all the winnings in the floor safe and live cheaply for one week. Then I would buy a couple of suits. "Remind me to call Richard Carroll's tomorrow," I shouted into the next room. "I want to order a couple of suits but I'm going to live like a monk this week. Maybe check the ponies again Thursday. Maybe Friday."

We ate dinner quietly. A fog floated just above my upstairs patio and the beaming red channel-entrance markers glistened like stars from another solar system through the undulating haze.

In bed with a glass of Lancer's Rosé in her hand, Elizabeth said, "I wanted to come over last night. In the worst way. I was reading this thick novel—*The Only Woman,* it was called—and this guy was loving up the heroine so terrifically that I thought I wouldn't be able to catch my breath." She put my hand onto her inner thigh and pulled herself close to me. "I should have run over. The pills make me crazy anyway."

"Listen," I said, "what were you doing at the track today?"

She leaped as if struck. The wine spilled. Blue eyes narrowed. I had expected them to widen. She set the glass down very deliberately and licked her hand. Maybe sex isn't everything, but she made it seem that way. When we made love the only two confessions she made were that she was four pounds too heavy and that she loved sex. It was a challenge.

"You didn't see me. I know you didn't."

"I don't have to. I have radar. Give me an answer."

"Why is it your business?"

"It just is. You and someone else kept the hair on the back of my neck raised. I didn't like it."

Her Bain de Soleil–tanned cheekbones flushed. "There was nothing to it. I just wanted to see you in your own environment. I wanted to know everything there is to know about you while you were unaware. I wanted to take care of you. It was nothing, really. I was going to——"

"Doing anything in relationship to my life while I am unaware frightens me. I don't need taking care of. This house is in perfect order—without a maid—and so am I, without a cook and bottle washer."

"I was going to come up to you and join you."

"After the big race?"

"Yes. You were involved in such an . . . inner way that I thought you had swallowed the world."

"Now tell me what I want to know. About the girl. I know you know, otherwise I wouldn't have been chosen."

She turned and lay flat on her back. She had a body that not only wouldn't stop, it never took a recess. And probably never would. It was painful to look at her and just talk.

"Hank Selmon called me," she said. "He asked me to come out. Said that he wanted to talk to me about a roommate. I told him I didn't want one, but he insisted I go out to the track and talk to him. So I did." She shrugged. "It gave me a chance to spy on you."

"You knew Mary Jarn, too."

"Yes. In a distant way."

"What does that mean?"

"She was Hank's sister. I knew Hank. That's all. . . . I hardly knew them Harvey," she said. "Honestly. I'm sorry about Mary, but I didn't know much about them."

"Somehow I have the feeling that everybody knows about everything except me."

"I'll tell you what I saw. Mary backed away from that regal looking lady. Pulled right out of her hands, then went over to you; the race started and everyone stood up and she disappeared. That's it." She looked at the ceiling, out into the night, then at me, eyes turning and resting calmly on mine in the half-moon light that filtered into the room. "My guess was that she sat down at your table. She was horribly pale. Like a china dish that had been painted on."

"The lady. Old? Young? Name?"

"Don't know her. Never saw her before. Maybe 35. Could be younger. But sort of elegant. Dark hair. Slim. Tall. That's about all. She was gone when I turned around."

She had to know it was Sylvia Sarafin, yet held back. "OK. One more favor."

"C'mon Harv. No more questions."

"Just one more. I want to know about Walter Sarafin, Hank's boss."

"Oh, god. Leave me alone. I sat through dinner while you were in another world. Now we're in bed and my time with you is taken up with your mysteries."

I waited in the dark.

"He seems to own Henry. That's all I know."

———◆———

Out on the beach someone with a rifle was waiting for me.

I found out later from Lew Mackin that I was targeted for a hit that night, but that I never got near a window—no place where a silhouette could be fixed long enough for an absolutely certain rifle shot.

I put my fingers on one of her nipples. She shuddered. I kissed her and began to pull my tongue down her torso, slowly, and she reached for me. Then we connected and rolled together, trying to get closer and yet closer. I needed it. To get lost in someone and her get lost in me. She began to gasp rhythmically. "Harvey!" I held on. I didn't want it to stop. Ever.

5

It wasn't my business to go chasing down Newport addresses, or trying to find out what and who killed Mary Jarn. I couldn't help it if I had an inside advance on the coroner's report. Doc Pinner had called me on the first Sunday after the death of Mary.

"It was Orinase, Harv. A proprietary synthetic insulin in pill form."

"What's that mean?"

"It's different than insulin, but the same idea. She either took too much of it, or somebody forced it into her."

"Keep going, simply and slowly, Doc."

"Well, she wasn't a diabetic . . . she shouldn't even know about Orinase, much less possess it. Too much will cause your pancreas to jump like crazy and create insulin. You go into a state of shock and then it kills you. And that's what happened."

"Why are you calling and telling me all of this?"

"You knew her, didn't you? I just thought you would want to know. It wasn't a nice way to die." I could picture his pudgy fingers poking holes in the air for emphasis.

"I didn't know her, didn't want to know, and don't want to be involved, Doc. I told you that."

I could just see his face. He would be frowning now with deep wrinkles spoiling his forehead, and the short

fingers of his left hand would start to tap his left cheek.
"OK, Harv, OK, but . . ."

"You don't believe me."

"Right. I don't believe you. I would like to, but I
don't."

"There must be a reason for not believing me, Doc.
Wouldn't you say?"

"Good-bye, Harvey."

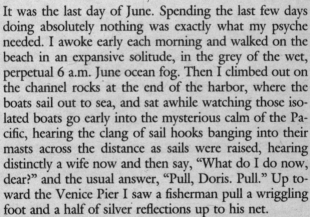

It was the last day of June. Spending the last few days
doing absolutely nothing was exactly what my psyche
needed. I awoke early each morning and walked on the
beach in an expansive solitude, in the grey of the wet,
perpetual 6 a.m. June ocean fog. Then I climbed out on
the channel rocks at the end of the harbor, where the
boats sail out to sea, and sat awhile watching those isolated boats go early into the mysterious calm of the Pacific, hearing the clang of sail hooks banging into their
masts across the distance as sails were raised, hearing
distinctly a wife now and then say, "What do I do now,
dear?" and the usual answer, "Pull, Doris. Pull." Up toward the Venice Pier I saw a fisherman pull a wriggling
foot and a half of silver reflections up to his net.

Then I went in, made breakfast, and took a nap. Awoke
again just before noon and saw a thousand sails leaning
into the green sea, which rustled like a windswept expanse
of Midwest grassland. In the afternoon I studied the *Daily
Racing Form*. I wrote in my journal. It was an old habit.
On this last June day at 2:30 p.m., I wrote:

> I suppose it's fate. I shouldn't be thinking about
> that girl. But she has stuck in my head and I walk
> in the morning mist and think of her. I also think
> that she has contrived to point a finger at me. Every-

thing seems to be pointing to me and I don't have a notion in the world why.

I am going to the races and win again. It gets rid of the tension. Maybe I'll lose. I don't care. Elizabeth is coming soon. I think of Kimberly often and Margaret now and then, but I know solitude is the only safe place for me.

6

———— ◆ ————

"Please come over," Tony said. "I've gotta talk to some-one. It's too much for me anymore. I'm just an old pug. You understand, Harvey?"

"I'll be there."

When I first met Tony Antonnini, he spent the evening drinking, screaming instructions to one of his fighters from the white corner, and playing the piano. That was long after his fighter had lost, long after the screaming. He played softly, incongruously, with a sense of melan-choly, as if everything was soon ending. That's the best explanation of the way he played; as if he would never play again. He played for himself. Booze put him into a special place and music transported him from there to the end of our curving universe and back deep into his. It was as if he had done something too awful to stay with, or as if it were yet to come.

His voice had been holding on by a string the last few years. It kept coming at you like wind through a rusty screen door.

"You know what?" he said to me that night, "I think I'm invulnerable. Nothing can get to me." He was wrong, of course.

Early that first night he squatted ringside and jabbed furiously at the air. His fighter was getting hit in the body and his gut gave like a bale of flour. In the third round

Tony's boy took a punch under the heart, and the lights and the misery and the sweat came together, and he reeled in slow motion to the canvas like a discarded banana peel, eyes open, waiting for the count. When it was over, Tony curled his thick arm about the boy and dusted him with a sponge. Then he turned and hollered up to the second aisle, "Hey, Roberto. Fighting is for fools—*es verdad,* eh? Only fools get in that box. Ah, redhead," he said to his fighter, "you are a fool. Ya' know?"

Then he said, to himself, but two rows could hear him, "This is a crazy game; lemme tell ya." He jerked a half pint of Wild Turkey from his jeans and downed a large gulp. "No one with brains would want to be in it now."

Later on that evening, long ago, I followed him to Sandy's Bar and Grille, in the midst of a street left over from the sixties, and he took over from the hired piano player, and I sat at the piano and we talked between numbers until the booze accumulated its effects like blows to his middle and he had to be led away.

I recalled that night as I stepped hurriedly up the concrete steps of his porch. The late-afternoon air dropped heavily over his weathered frame house: grey, chipped pillars and creaking front porch, a circa-1925 structure that is original Southern California. In the East one found smaller porches and second stories and tons of brick. In Chicago you saw asbestos siding and chocolate brick—and next to the highway, in Philadelphia and Cincinnati, all the same. But here wood lasted as long as the termites would let it, and designers developed a kind of sloped-roof, chipped-rock look that was uniquely local. You could peg a neighborhood's heyday from the color of its clapboard.

The house was just around the corner from L'Orangerie Restaurant. Once in a while I treated myself to its elegant service and cuisine.

Tony shoved the dusty, screeching screen door open

and nervously flipped a dead cigarette past me and motioned. "I know. I know, kid. I been drinkin'. But just a little. I've been off a long time." His throat was raspier than usual, as if it had been slugged. His eyes were almost crazy. Their color had faded to milk and into his faded soul. His shoulders jerked and he breathed quickly through his nose. "You know, I won a lotta fights in my day. I wasn't any slouch. Not just a club rummy. You know, kid?"

"Yes, Tony, I know. You were first-rate." I hated it when he was drinking. "Now tell me why I'm here."

"You think I could take you now? You got the reach but you're skinny. Whadaya think, Harv?"

"I'm also big in the shoulders, and you know I can take you or you would have tried a long time ago." I looked at him squarely. He had grown a little heavy. But not much. His hair had receded. Wisps of grey stuck out into the air. Eyes were reddened but not just from drinking. Secrets pressed out from behind the guilt in his eyes. "I know you've helped me a lot, Harv. But don't look at me like that. You've got all the wrong reasons."

"I'll listen . . . if that's all you want."

"Here. I'll getcha a beer. We'll sit over a beer like when we were just kids."

"I was already an old man when I first met you, Tony. I was a genuine, hired-patriot, red-blooded, American kidnap-and-kill artist then."

He avoided my pique and got a beer from his box, and lowered his formidable frame onto a green leatherette recliner. My dad used to do that, I remembered. Come home and throw his shoes in the front door and get a beer, and sit in his favorite chair. But he wasn't built like Tony. He was tall, almost slight, and had a bad limp, and wore a blond mustache, and seldom smiled. And he lectured a great deal—"You must *always*——this or that. *Never* do——" And he was so distant. And I sometimes wanted just to touch him but could not. I recalled that he said he always told the truth. No matter what. He was perfect and godly. I knew he was perfect because my mother always laughed, said it was so, and then laughed again.

Tony's voice brought me back into an anxious present. "OK. OK, Harv. OK." He sighed and dragged on his beer. Standing up, he waved his hands and slopped the drink onto the carpeting. He looked down into the faded designs and grimaced as if he had broken a brittle and prized possession. "Damn, the beer gets to me, doesn't it?" Then he shrugged. "It always did. Listen . . . I want to hire you, Harvey. On a regular business basis. No friendship or that stuff. I can afford it." He was poised over me. "Don't worry. I can afford it like you wouldn't believe." His steamy eyes rolled. "But I need you. And you're the only one left."

"I don't hire out anymore, Tony. You know that. I don't want anything to do with death anymore. Besides, there's no indispensable man—I'm not even sure I want to hear your story."

"I'm gonna tell you, no matter what. You're gonna have to listen."

Pulling myself up, I went to his Coldspot and cracked open my own beer. "I don't know about foresight and hindsight," I said, "but I quit. A long time ago."

Margaret used to wait for me, I thought, playing with Kim on the warm carpet of our westside stucco house. Sometimes I would find them early the next morning asleep on the yellow couch—in a waiting pose.

"You can't quit, Harv. I can't even quit fighting. What you *do* and what you *are* become the same after a while." He lit another cigarette then blinked and pushed the deep past from his mind.

"Harv, you gotta listen first and I've gotta show you something. Just don't say anything, don't say anything."

He waved his hand and his beer foamed around his fingers. "Don't say anything. Just wait. Just listen. You're my friend and you'll do it."

"I'm listening."

"You know my boy William?"

I nodded. "Of course."

"He's a good kid. You know that, Harvey Ace, you son of a bitch," he said in a restrained, playful way. "It has to do with him. And—" he shook his head like an ancient lion, "and it has to do with lots of other things I'm gonna confess to you, Harv."

"I don't like the idea. Not at all." I didn't tell him what Lew had said about reporting me as involved in Mary Jarn's kidnapping.

He pulled at my sleeve, gingerly. The same old tugging. I knew I didn't want to know. He led me to his bedroom closet. There was a brass cornered foot locker in it the size of a double suitcase. He grasped a brown slipper from the upper shelf, slipped a key out of the inner sole and unlocked the case. World War II uniforms and painful memories were neatly folded inside. He reached in and strained and pulled out a large steel box.

"This is it, Harv. I never needed all those horses. I don't feel bad, though, 'cause this is for William. It's not really mine." A quiet inner resolve had come over him. The edge of drunkenness peeled away from his eyes and voice. "I didn't need your horses, Harv. But I used them because, look——" He opened the box. Stacks of $20 and $50 packets in geometric piles glistened like green blood.

"It's not exactly Kleenex, is it?" I said, quietly.

He pushed his nose close to mine, jerking out a handkerchief from his hip pocket and dabbing his eyes as if they belonged to a weepy child. He was crying in his head and in his heart, not sobbing. "It's $800,000, Harvey. It's a real—no counterfeit—$800,000. You could spend it today." Then he laughed nervously. "Well?"

I turned, avoiding eggshells in my mind, and collapsed into his overstuffed couch.

"I didn't want to use the money, Harv. It's for William. I always kept it for him. He needs it."

"Tony, stop for a minute. Close the box." I waved my finger.

He did, and placed it tenderly next to me.

"No more beer. No more bourbon. Nothing. Pour some of that coffee I smell—for both of us—and start from the beginning. From absolute scratch."

Even though he was ten to twelve years my senior, I had been a father figure for at least that long a time. He obeyed, and as I heard the cups clatter, a shudder of death uncoiled in me. One might think that so much money would be a breath of life, but it hadn't made Anthony Antonnini content. It had obviously consumed his every waking moment.

He served the coffee in delicate, gold laced bone china from a silvery tray. "This was my wife's prize," he said, nodding at the set. "She liked this sort of thing. Sterling silver too. Syl didn't like——" he stopped.

I sighed. "C'mon, let's have it. Tell me the whole thing."

It was dark in the house. Its sounds came alive. Scratching and groaning gently. I heard a siren wail from up near Santa Monica Boulevard where there was always a happening. In today's L.A. it was a street of constant happenings.

"This is the way it was. . . . Henry and I made a killing, a big one. Henry Selmon. I knew his dad, he was a fight promoter. Not big, mind you. Club stuff. At the old Hollywood Legion and the Ocean Park Arena, and some better bouts at the Olympic. Made a living, you know. That's what he did. And along came this runty wise-ass kid who wanted nothin' but money. Everything was money. Jack Selmon's kid." He shook his head. "I liked Jack. . . ." The story came from unknown distances in the past. "Hank knew everyone. That kid had a way. He smiled, and the whole track lit up. He was a lover boy, too. Ladies crawled over themselves for this skinny thing. He was dark and sleek-like, then, mind you. But temperamental. God, was he temperamental."

"Get on with it."

"OK. Well, finally he married Sylvia. She was something else. It wasn't just looks. She oozed promises from her hips. Brother. But she didn't have that soft look like most of those girls. She had an edge. One day he came to me and told me he had this big transaction. We had made a few small deals . . . bringing in dope from Mexico. It was easy. From Caliente to Del Mar to L.A. and wherever. The big risk is breaking the stuff down and getting it onto the streets. That's for wholesalers and retailers, not suppliers. This time Hank said we had a ten million dollar 'transaction.' I didn't understand it. He was doing OK at the track. No Ralph Neves or John Longdon, but he did OK. Anyway, Hank made the deal. We were getting $10 million. Ten million dollars! I couldn't get the amount clear in my mind. Can you imagine? A million junkies at $10 a pop?"

"How does an old fighter fit in? What could you do for Hank Selmon?"

"Whadaya mean? I'm the guy that made all those deals go. I'm the guy who did it. I was the brains." He was insulted. He had stopped the booze and was on the still hot coffee.

"They had the connection. You think I'm nothing. But I never was. You saw me on the way down. But when I was a kid, I was good. Northeastern Conference Boxing Champ—Syracuse. You think you know me? I wasn't just a club fighter, ya know." His voice got raspier and he kept stabbing his finger and building up steam.

I sat quietly and kept still.

He sighed and finished his narrative of what had happened six years ago. When he stopped fighting he lived on his luck. He flew junkets to Vegas and filled in on the keyboard now and then, and got his instrument license and hung around local airports, picking up gamblers and flying them to Golden Gate, to Las Vegas, or down to Caliente. He hung around with me on his "off-times."

When Hank Selmon approached him to make the arrangements for a couple of hundred bricks of marijuana and maybe 50 or 100 pounds of cocaine, it was easy for him to set it up. He became Hank's man. And then Hank became Tony's man.

Tony made all the arrangements, but this time they were loading up tons of marijuana and dozens of half-liter sacks of cocaine. The entire West Coast could fly on that load—30 million dollars' worth. Even the Feds and the locals knew that somehow, someplace soon, a huge load was coming in.

Everything was done very carefully. Tony checked the plane, the flight plan, the weight of the load, the length of the field going and coming in.

When the plane landed with its cargo in the California desert, Mary Selmon, who had been held hostage to ensure the completion of Hank's part of the bargain, was released to him. Mary, who William Antonnini had come to adore as an adolescent without a female around the house, was the fulcrum of the transaction. Everything balanced on who was in control of her destiny and when. After her release, all hell broke loose. Walter Sarafin's bodyguard killed the pilot. They all ran for the cases of money. Tony got to them first and leveled Sarafin's bodyguard with "my best shot ever. A left hook from the knees." In the confusion, Tony managed to get one case of goods and to get Henry and Mary into their car.

As the story unraveled, I realized that in some strangely twisted, remote way I had been involved in Mary's life for a long time. Now her death.

"That's how it was, Harvey. Henry ran off with his sister, and I grabbed the case."

"And Mary . . . what happened to her?"

"I told you. She went with Henry."

"What else?" I needed to know more. "Did you know her?"

"Yeah."

"So OK, tell me what she was like."

"Harv, she was like, well, sort of like lost . . . y'know? But she was a terrific girl. Terrific."

"More," I urged.

"It's hard. She wasn't easy to know. Sort of far away, if you know what I mean. Yeah, far away. Like she had gauze over her black eyes." He grew silent.

"And?"

"We all got away. I worked out a sale, and there's my share."

"What else?"

"Nothin'. Plain nothin'."

"And Bill?"

"He watched over Mary. He got—you know kids— he got fond of her. But she just ignored him. She made him crazy thinking about her. Then she got married, and William, he sort of grew up. And that's all . . . except William is missing. Gone. Just like Mary disappeared before that last big hit."

7

A sudden breeze came up and annoyed the curtains around the greying, flaking, work-worn living room windows. The material was as thin as the skin of a very old lady and twisted in the entrails of the wind helplessly. Tony's skin sagged drearily around his eyes and chin. He looked at me. "I'm tired as a Golden Glover in his first six-rounder. But I have to get it out. I need your help."

"First tell me how you had the guts to keep the money around all this time? I only read about things like this in the newspapers."

"Listen, Harv. Just tell a waiter in Mazatlán or Acapulco or stop a kid in Hermosillo. Tell him you want a little smoke and flash money, and you can buy 50 pounds of anything within 10 minutes. Shipments like mine are regular things. The real dealers have timetables, flight times, regular crews. Well," he sighed and rubbed his nose with a left knuckle, "you're going to love this."

"I'm sure."

His balding pate wrinkled. The fuzz around his ears seemed electrified. He smiled. "I kept the money in a safe deposit box, hid the key in *your* house and gave Cyril Weber a letter telling the whole story and told him to open it only if something not so kosher—" he waved his hand as if balancing a marble on the back of it—"happened to me. And then I made a mistake and told Selmon that one of the keys was in your house."

My lower intestine squeezed itself into a great colicky pain. "You son of a bitch. What have you done to my life? I've been living on borrowed time all these years?"

"You were as safe as I was. Hank always thought you were my brains anyway."

I pressed myself tightly beneath the rib cage, and leaned forward and breathed evenly. Antonnini's voice broke into the dark room.

"I taped the key to the bottom of the water-tank lid in your guest bathroom, and I tossed the second key onto the floor of your garage in the middle of the dirt and oil, and just kicked it into the corner. It's still there. . . . Your key I got back last year. Cyril Weber, the lawyer, and I talked about it, and I felt safe and I liked the idea of living with the money around. It's mine. Every penny." His eyes glistened. Then milk descended over them. The wind died.

He tilted close to me. The faded sweet scent of Tequila Gold drifted into my nose. "William is gone, Harvey." He took a breath and waited for it to sink in. "William is missing. He disappeared three days ago. His bed is still unmade. He hasn't been at school. I've called his close friends and they haven't seen him. I don't know if they're really close friends. He doesn't have many friends, I don't think. But he's tough, Harvey. Quiet and tough. I couldn't take him."

William was a well-scrubbed and solitary young man. He had a quality of threatening stillness and a quality of special affection for his father that was only now and then apparent—"Come home soon, dad, please"—which you saw in his obscure eyes. He was twenty-two now and finishing his senior year on a cinema scholarship and state loans at Cal State, Northridge. He had long since ceased burdening Tony with the need for money. His every movement seemed carefully planned. Difficult things came so simply to him that you knew they had been carefully practiced.

"Is there any reason, Tony? After all, he's twenty-two and never had to report."

"But he always *did*. That's the point. No phone call. No note. Nothing.. Like I said before, it's unreal. Something is wrong. He just disappeared. You have to find him." He reached over to the box, moving into and out of the lamplight as he counted small packets of twenties. It seemed as if he was moving into and out of life and that William was the ineffable force keeping his soul from staying on the dead side of the line.

The refrigerator motor stopped and left a heavy silence. My heart beat high in my throat.

"Find him," Tony repeated, clearing his throat. "Here's ten thousand. I never spent a penny of it till now." He dropped the package onto my lap.

"I'm not touching this money until you tell me more. I need to know more."

"William is missing and I can't find Hank Selmon. He told me a week ago that he got a call from Sylvia. From out of the blue. Out of the dark past. Then suddenly, Hank is gone. Maybe she's got something going about this money. I don't know. Maybe she found out about it. Whatever Hank knows, Sylvia knows. They didn't hate each other when they split. But I know when I'm not safe. We're not safe anymore, Harv. Not anymore."

I sat back and fingered through the bills. The curtains danced in the fickle breeze, and shadows fluttered at my feet. Nothing seemed real except the dead girl, the money, and what Tony Antonnini wanted from me. "You've probably ruined our lives, my friend. We may not live through this thing. It *feels* bigger than a suitcase of money and one murder."

He ran a row of knuckles across his nose again. "Listen.

Let's have another drink. I've been good with liquor for weeks. I'm tired of worrying about booze. Whadaya say?"

I put the bills in my pocket. Then I went into his bathroom, looked at my face in a mirror that had a yellow swath cutting through its middle. My eyelids bulged from weariness and my chin was narrower than the last time I had looked. After splashing water on my face and neck and pressing my temples, I went to William's room. Tony was on my tail. There was a 35mm Nikkomat on the dresser, and a filtered telescope lens hanging on the wall. Nothing was disturbed. Piles of photographs covered the twin canvas chairs.

There was nothing apparent. Tony kept getting in my way whenever I turned. "It's been interesting, Mr. Antonnini," I said, lightly. "But I'm tired and I need to ask you a lot more questions." I made a date for the next evening.

Experience made me know that Tony was being watched. Instincts made me know that I was being watched, too. It explained the shivers I felt as I walked to my car. Tony rushed out raising his fist—"Find my boy!"

The breeze curled dust into circles as I drove. Moonbeams caught the funnels and turned them into dancing ashes. That disturbed choreography made it difficult to see when I reached the driveway of my house.

Only in retrospect can one see that certain happenings were meant to be. It may be that life is already written and that the secret is kept only from the living. I rolled this idea over in my mind as I drifted off to sleep and to my dreams of buried horrors.

8

♦

Just before awakening, I was certain I heard a tapping at the glass door below. I reached for my gun and realized that I never slept with it anymore. I grabbed it from the drawer, searched out toward the delicious dawn blue sea, and gave it up as a part of my dreams. Coffee was a godsend. The smell was beyond sensuality. I took the pot into the alcove adjoining my den and began to sift through my indexed files. Tony's name led me to Harriet, his deceased wife, and Harriet to her mother and father whose last address was in lower Manhattan. William's card read: "Photographer, ROTC, transferred high schools, senior year."

I was led to Henry Selmon's card, which read: "Former jockey—now training. Volatile. Good with hands. Sister, Mary. Father, Jack Selmon—deceased. Boxing promoter. Hangs out at George's Bar and Grill, Inglewood. License for pistol. Suspected dealing with street dope. Wife . . . Sylvia. Well-traveled. Jet Set history. Check with Tony. Born year earlier than Henry, in '51. Miami, Florida. Remarried. Selmon trains for W.S. Stables; Sarafin, Incorporated."

Check with Tony?

Then Elizabeth Hume: "Born 1946, Glendale Community Hospital. Mother, nurse. Father, school principal. Pasadena Rose Princess. Married; *Michael Jarn,* second marriage 1968–69. School teacher, Westgate School, Flintridge."

"Check with Tony," kept twirling through my cranium. When I told him that we were surrounded by something bigger, I wasn't aware of the Elizabeth Hume connection. I created a Michael Jarn card for the files cross-indexed to Mary Jarn, then to Anthony Antonnini. Then I checked Sarafin as the sun crept higher into the eastern air. All I had on file was that Walter Sarafin was born in Turkey in 1929 and traveled to the Near East regularly. No source material. Just a note.

I showered and strapped myself into a holster and slipped my .38 into it. After a half-glass of orange juice, I washed my hands again and left.

It was still early and sunlight made everything in the morning haze fuzzy and foreboding. Dark glasses cut the haze, but not the foreboding. In two minutes the digital clock would say 7:30. The car felt good. No cold coughing and wheezing. Still young at heart. Traffic was building up on the freeway north into West Los Angeles, and then to the central part of town. Angelenos loved to bitch and moan while they threaded their asphalt arteries to work each morning. But they wouldn't trade for a bus and couldn't trade for a train. It was a town of 200 square miles without a rail transit system, it was a town where every car was a castle. I tried listening to Dave Brubeck on the tape and then to the news and finally settled for quiet. The faces of my fellow drivers were serene. I remembered again an old thesis I was positive I had originated: in spite of bitching and moaning, cars were a last refuge—the last indefatigable castle.

I knew what I was going to do. As I noticed the Orange County airport off to the right of the freeway, the sun broke through. I wanted to check the note but remembered that I had left it on my desk—it wasn't important. I had written the address in my mind . . . 201 Walnut,

Newport Beach. "The Taurus Connection," I think it said.

I also thought, "Someone, somehow, knows I'm coming. I'm not being followed. But my steps are known, predictable."

I turned off at Jamboree Road and headed into Newport. The highway wound around the brown-yellow hills and past the cement and wet green of the University of California, Irvine, and then past the fancy Newporter Inn. The tennis courts were already in use . . . on a Tuesday. No one works in Southern California. The good life.

And I thought, I *must* go to the address, I had no choices. I would be careful. There was a dragging at my heart. I breathed deeply, wanting to think beyond my silent hunters. I wanted to turn every fact over again. But it came out the same—I would have to put the puzzle together before the unknown others did or I would get into a dead condition.

I turned right on Pacific Coast Highway. Along the road, Transpac Yacht Sales were jammed between a Mama's Burgers and a sail-rigging shop. An architect's office, Burdette Weiner; a three-story apartment house with dark-wood balconies overlooking the jungle of Balboa Bay; the Sea Scouts office; Mike's Hobie Cat Showroom; Captain Nemo's Water Bed and Pillow Shoppe; The Chart House for steaks, the Grinder for more burgers; the pillared and manicured, green-thumbed entrance to the Balboa Bay Club; Newport Pacific Boat Yards with the bow of a lush forty-footer hanging nearly into the street; then Captain's Liquor Locker; the Kawasaki Center; Sally's Antique establishment; Lydia's Interiors; Anchorage Yacht Sales with a half-finished blue schooner looming above the red roof line. There were Hobie Cats and Skip Jacks and Bayliners in the midst of Datsuns and Hondas, the Art Center and the Neptune Society. There was a sign that read, "Have a little fun tonight," and above it the sign also read, "Neighborhood Massaging Parlour and Snack Shop."

I drove past a marshy area known as the Back Bay, then left onto Balboa peninsula through the middle of the area's best showroom apartments and new restaurants.

Near the Balboa Bay ferry I came to Walnut Street, on the ocean side of Balboa Boulevard; 201 Walnut was a pink-stucco, six-unit structure. I went around the block once and then through the alley. Nothing unusual.

A quarter of an hour of staring changed nothing, except my mind was clearer and focused on pictures of how to reach for my gun quickly, how to dive and roll and shoot at the same time, and how to use my weight to dump someone who came up behind me.

I looked at the mailbox. The front apartment had the name Jarn on it, then a dash and the name Antonnini. The same dragging on my heart started again.

I decided not to ring the doorbell. The door was open. There were smells. Every scent is accentuated by proximity to the sea. Cigarette smoke attacks you. Cooking carries its dripping odors beneath your eyelids. The apartment had been inhabited recently. Heart thumping jammed my ears. I left the door open. A cheap chrome and red formica kitchen set stood like a bad painting next to the kitchen door. The bedroom door was ajar. My eyes singled out a black oxford propped up on the floor next to the bed. Then there was a foot, and a leg, and everything else—icy hands and face hanging from a pin-striped grey suit. Eyes stared at the ceiling. I guessed that they used to do their seeing for Cyril Weber.

The room had been ransacked, not hurriedly, but professionally. In fact, it seemed like it had just happened. I touched Weber's hand to see if it was still warm. It was. I knew suddenly that there was much more to Tony's story. And in that same silent instant, my breath caught in my throat, electricity turned me "on." Without really hearing, I "heard" the presence.

A trouser leg came at me and then a flash and a vague, painful awareness that more blows were falling. I kept my mind on one thing—my gun. I pulled it and squeezed the trigger and felt the noise shudder through me. It was a quiet moment, and I began to see light and fired again. I was hit in the thigh and rolled to the other side and fired toward where the pain was coming. Now I could see fuzzily. The room traveled. It bent foolishly, and I wanted to shoot at it as if a bullet would stop the craziness. There were shadows. Hands above me. I did not shoot again but pulled back and lurched down onto the bed. I knew there was hot blood on my face and neck. I said to myself, "Let it not be mine. Dammit, I don't want it to be mine."

In a moment I was able to survey the room without wanting to vomit. An almost fat, blond fellow, very thick around the neck and shoulders, perhaps thirty-five years old, lay on his side, gurgling air. Then it stopped. He had been hit twice, once in the right groin and once in the right chest. I felt lacerations behind my left ear and above both eyes and a heaviness in my thigh. I must have been kicked in the forehead and the right hip.

Experience saved my life. There was a two-foot club in the man's hands, but no gun. He must have thought that stealth was his best weapon. I began to search the floor for his gun. I was certain that it had been blown away from him by the impact of my initial bullet. I felt under the dresser and shoved the bed away from the wall. Then a car screamed at me and away—a Porsche; I could tell by the whine. Two people, either together or separately, had visited Cyril Weber—or had been visited by him.

I stumbled to the door. A wrinkled lady wrapped in a baby-blue housecoat and with inky long hair hanging dryly to her shoulders said in a nasal whine, "Is anything wrong?"

"Nothing, ma'am," I replied like Jack Webb, and shoved my gun back into its place. "Call the police. Go inside and call the cops." That would keep her from following me and seeing my car. She obeyed, and I managed to climb in, and got away quietly. I was sure a dozen people had seen me. There always were.

Even though I was wet and sick I stayed on the freeway heading back. In a while I drove off the road and stopped at a Mobil station. The bathroom door was open and I took a look at myself. I would be fifty-five years old on Pearl Harbor Day and up until two weeks ago was living the easy life. I had been missing only one thing—being closer to my daughter. That's particularly why I took Tony's money. I know how he felt about William. Love isn't the right word. Sometimes a kid gets under your skin so insistently, so deep into your gut, that it transcends life.

Now I was beat up, looking like a sick drunk. I was flailing about in the middle of a puzzle that had more loose ends than a dish of linguini. And I had just killed someone. It was sinking in. I had killed someone again—after such a long time. I was not like Raven in "This Gun for Hire." It *meant* something to me. I didn't know the dead man, and he was undoubtedly trying to kill me. But it didn't matter. I let go and sobbed it out.

9

───────♦───────

"Have you seen Hank Selmon?" I asked Don Lennock, a regular Hot Walker who moved as if he was in water all the time.

"He ain't been around, Mr. Ace. Go see Jim—over there. By Mr. Binder's stable. He may know. By the way. What hit you?"

I had driven down to Del Mar, cutting off the freeway and heading down into the former marsh field where the old track nestled. I moved a car length at a time past the dusty acres of parking, along the pink-stucco wall that closed in the barns and the racetrack. This racetrack was intimate. You could smell the horses and fodder from the roadway. Not like Santa Anita and Hollywood Park, where the horses never seemed to need wiping from the dust and where every inch was paved except for explosions of flowers strewn about the oval inside of the running track. I turned into the valet parking area, gave Sasha Lopez a five-dollar bill, and stuffed my car between the limos at the Turf Club gate. The Crosby exhibition hall to the south was like a graceless hothouse cramping the scurrying attendants into breathless near misses.

Inside, the old Spanish porticos were unaware of the sleeveless crowd they enveloped. A lazy atmosphere rose. Casual costumes bloomed like moving bougainvillae. Horses were already circling the saddling oval. Jocks, owners, and trainers murmured among themselves as the crowds leaned on white fences. I pushed into the circle and through it, smiling as if I was the track steward. Trying to be pleasant, I shoved through the entrance gateway to the stable area. That's when Lennock told me to check with Jim Bradford.

"It can't be Harvey Ace," Bradford smiled broadly, with the creases on his red, freckled face deepening as he viewed my skid row condition. "What happened, Harv?"

"Tripped in one of the stables, Jim. Spooked one of your crazy animals."

"Don't knock the poor creatures, Harvey, they're a living for both of us."

"I take it all back. But I can read their minds, and I know what they're thinking."

"Oh, oh. Here it comes. I've probably heard it before."

"No you haven't. No jokes today. Just got myself scared to death and a little beat up. Say, have you seen Hank Selmon around?"

He told me that Hank was last seen on Sunday; that he had a winner for Walter Sarafin; that he was certain that Hank had been with Sylvia.

I thanked him, walked through a line of animals that were cooling down, blustering softly as they were gentled back to reality. Grooms clucked and talked as if to infants. The irregular thudding of hooves signaled the anticipation of ready thoroughbreds. They knew when it was time for them to race. Some were born losers, like poor people in the Place and Show lines or the quiet gentlemen in the box seats who beat themselvs to death by losing more than money. Some were honest, who wanted to win and sometimes did and almost always gave it a good try. A few were winners who still lost half of the time, like good surgeons and trial lawyers who lost because they were willing to play the game.

At Walter Sarafin's stable area I looked around and saw

two men dressed in pinstriped business suits and brown oxfords. They weren't gambling men and were unaccustomed to horses and dust and hay. I asked one of the grooms if Sarafin was nearby.

Walter Sarafin was tall and grey. Distinguished. He was this side of sixty-five years, most of which he had run exactly as he chose. I watched. He nodded his head and a chestnut colt came out of a stall and began walking in slow circles. His attention was on everything at once; eyes never still.

"I don't know that much about him," Jim told me. "He's usually gone except for a couple of weeks in the winter at Santa Anita and a few weeks here at Del Mar. Hank runs his stable. Been doing it for six or seven years."

I found out where Sarafin lived, then left and called Tony to tell him I couldn't meet him for dinner. I wanted to ask him about his keeping an apartment at Newport Beach and about the name Jarn. A big voice in my gut told me to keep it all to myself. It was a rule. The more I found out and the less anyone else found out, the better off I'd be.

10

♦

I beat closing time at a men's store in La Jolla. I brought pearl-grey slacks and two shirts, and while the tailor did a quick hemming job on the slacks and pressed my new shirts, I gathered a bucket of toiletries and some good soap and a small attaché case from Nickerman's Drugs. Parking lots were disgorging their rolling cargo onto green shaded avenues. A salty mist began to dance lightly over the ruffled palm trees. I checked in at the Sea View Hotel, which had only one side with a sea view. Old French doors opened to a miniature balcony looking north. The grinning phosphorescent waves curved away from sight. The wind was grey and foreboding.

I dialed Sam Rosenstock.

"Sam? It's me, Harvey Ace. I'm sorry to bother you, Sam——."

"Oh, hiya, Ace," he interrupted in a suspicious tone. "To what do I owe this pleasure?"

"Sam, I've got to talk to you . . . about that girl who was murdered, and about Tony. Anthony Antonnini. Things have been happening. I think I need your help."

His voice lowered. "Wait a minute . . . hold on." There was silence at the other end for a moment, as if he were moving into a corner. "OK. Go ahead. Tell me what's up. But I don't know how I can help you. *You're* the detective."

"Listen, Sam. You know pieces of history that can help me. I'm sure of it. And I think I'm in trouble. Maybe *real* trouble."

"Ace, I'm not a real cop," he said with a sudden flat candor. "I just play at it, shall we say. And I keep the drunks from messing up the place and keep the gangster types away from my park. That's all. I don't know why you're calling me."

"Sam, trust me. No involvement."

"That's right. That's just what I don't want. Involvement. With guys like you, Ace. You're too slick. I'm just a retired fighter who found a soft touch in his, shall we say, mellow years. I don't want to sort of slide into anything. You know how that can be. Suddenly you're in the middle of someone else's mess and you don't know how you got there."

"I know how that can be. But you know Tony pretty well. He's the one who is involved."

"I don't want to know what's going on, Harvey. I don't want to know more about Tony or you or Mary or William or anyone. Call Llewelyn Mackin at LAPD. I really don't know all that history. That's, shall we say, final."

"I don't get it. How do you know who I'm going to ask about?"

The phone shut me out. Click. Dead. I dialed again.

"Tony?"

"Yeah, kid?"

"You talked to Sam Rosenstock lately?"

"Naw. Why should I do that?"

"Don't give me a question for an answer. Have you been talking to Sam lately?"

"No."

"I've got a bushel of questions, friend. I think you better decide to tell me everything when I see you."

"Just tell me if you found Bill. The rest is nothing."

"I'll find him."

"Wait, Harv——."

I didn't.

I cleaned and checked my revolver, unbuckled the harness and put the whole set into a flap in the attaché case. I walked to Anthony's Grotto. They gave me a singleton quickly, and I sat among the tourists and fountains and seashells, and waited for above-average tourist fare while I nursed a J & B over the rocks. I felt better after the lobster and drove toward Torrey Pines along a two-lane coastal road.

Just a mile before reaching the extension of the golf course, I turned my Jag down a half-moon driveway, stopped and stared for a moment at the contemporary stretched-out house covered in ivy and protected by azaleas and holly bush all around. The spread covered a pad held into the air just above the angry green ocean by an invisible hand. A brick terrace and three-foot wall faced west. There was a Rolls in front of me. I saw lights through glass brick windows. I moved the car so that it found the exit, then took the ignition key and removed it from its key chain and shoved it into my left trouser pocket. The remainder of the keys I tossed on the seat. It was better than fumbling for the right key if I suddenly became rushed.

The door was answered by a pale woman with short grey hair. She weighed fifty pounds too much for her five-foot frame. She didn't smile.

"Yes?"

"I have an appointment with Mr. Sarafin. I'm Harvey Ace."

She looked at me suspiciously. "At this hour?"

"Don't worry. He'll see me."

She turned her head to look up at me. "I don't believe you, but I'll ask. I don't make the decisions."

"That's right," I replied. "You don't."

She wheeled away leaving a huff behind.

In a moment I heard a female voice. I stepped inside and the unhappy maid returned. "I didn't tell you to enter, did I? This house is guarded, Mr. Ace. We're very isolated here. There's a video system on all parts of the grounds."

"I appreciate the information," I replied lightly. "I sort of drifted in. On the way out I'll give your cameras a ten-second profile."

She turned disgustedly, "This way. Mrs. Sarafin is waiting in the den."

There was an antiseptic sort of smell in the air. Vaguely sweet. Tile floors clattered under her heel. The house was built completely around an interior garden, with an extra wing for the game room, den and living room, each open to the other but defined by stone and brick fireplaces. I caught my breath as I entered the game room. Oversized hunting trophies gaped at me with lustrous brown eyes. Antelope, deer, a water buffalo, a set of yellowing tusks, and a cluster of small heads that appeared to be dogs and wolves—possibly hyenas—they were all laughing at me.

"Mr. Ace?" The voice was low and inviting, but it seized me by its suddenness, and I whirled.

She was dark and elegant. Her hair curled easily and accentuated the angle and lift of her cheek bones. Her face was quietly lovely: tanned skin, distant dark eyes lidded by cool green mascara. She wore an aqua sheath over her revealed body. They were right: Sylvia Selmon had an intense appeal. If she wrapped herself around you, you might never be let go. Her eyes didn't stray.

"Hello, Mr. Ace. Do you remember me?" I shook my head. "Well, you're right," she nodded. "That was presumptuous of me. You would have no reason to remember." She waited a moment to make sure. "I was once wedded—lightly—to Henry Selmon. It seems like a thousand years ago." She hurried to get the preliminaries out of the way. "Walter and I have been married six years. April 22, it was. Second day of the sign of Taurus. I think it means that we're stuck with each other. Through thick or thin and whether we like it or not. Tauruses are like that." She smiled gently. I couldn't tell if it was gentle from resignation or from a sense of power.

"I don't think I've had the pleasure, Mrs. Sarafin. I do remember seeing you now and then around the track when Hank was riding. But we never met, otherwise I would know your birthdate, husband, all your addresses, mother's home phone number, and if you like mushu pork . . . and perhaps more."

"I take it that means you are a careful and thorough man," she said, and arched her head slightly as if to get another view of my nose.

"I am. It's sort of a hobby."

"Like horses," she smiled. She moved into the room and propped herself against the stone mantle of the fireplace. "You must know Henry pretty well, being involved in racing and all. Henry was good at everything, wasn't he? That's what I adored about him. He didn't need to be careful. That busy little body of his was everywhere. Loved everything . . . and everyone."

"So I've heard, but——."

"Oh," she laughed, "don't try to be kind. It's all history. I had one kind of life and now I have a new life, and——."

"And no memories."

Hesitation crept into her voice. "A few. But no regrets. Not enough time for regrets." She reached and caressed the brow of one of the fawn-colored dogs, then stopped and lit the gas pipe in the fireplace.

"Everyone has regrets. Even the bad guys."

She straightened, kindled by the fire, luminous. "Um . . . I suppose. If you give yourself time. But, you came here to see Walter, didn't you? Not to reminisce. He'll be here in a few moments. He's had a long day. Frustrating. It frustrates me, really. His affairs take him away so often." She said "affairs" as if the word was an enemy.

"Do you know where Hank is now?"

Her brow was streaked in thin crevices, suddenly showing her age. "I would think you are more informed than I am."

"That doesn't answer me." I felt as if each of us possessed something of value the other wanted.

"I don't owe you an answer, Mr. Ace. In any event, I don't——."

I interrupted. "Tell me about Mary Jarn." I detected a touch of please in my voice. "It can't hurt now to tell me about her, I mean . . ."

She held her breath, lips not exactly thinning, but pressed suddenly back against her teeth. It lasted only a moment. "She was—well, how can I explain?—special?"

Walter Sarafin entered just then and she looked up as if waiting for permission to continue, changed her mind and inquired, "Feeling better?"

His quiet demeanor seemed to take charge of a large space around him. Sylvia sunk into a deep red leather chair. He glanced at his wife first and nodded, and then to me with a vague trace of European gentility. But it wasn't that. He did not like to speak first. After the acknowledgement, he stood and waited for me to begin. I didn't. He was fitted snugly into a navy blue shirt and pants and white-buck shoes. Behind his light eyes, the wheels rolled.

"Yes, thank you, dear. I'm feeling much better," he replied, finally, and turned to me. "We weren't expecting visitors tonight, Mr. Ace."

"You look like you were."

"Mr. Ace is asking about Henry, Walter." Her voice had an edge. "You wouldn't be able to help him, would you?"

He moved to the opposite end of the room rather

stiffly, just below the head of a lovely buck with prize-winning antlers. "Is that why you're here, Mr. Ace?"

"Partly. And partly to find out about Mary Jarn. . . ."

"I think I'd like a sherry," Sarafin remarked. "You?"

I nodded and turned to Sylvia.

"No, Mr. Ace," she said. "I stay away from liquor and wines."

Sarafin eased to the open bar and poured the dark fluid into thinly blown, intricately woven, long-stemmed crystal glasses.

"Oh, Sylvia's not ill, though. Keeps herself in shape."

"I noticed," I said.

"Do you know where Hank is, Walter?" she persisted.

He turned away from her. "I presume wherever he is supposed to be. Now," directing his attention to me, "let's get on with this. I'd like to be polite——."

"You're doing well——."

"But you've disturbed my evening. So you want to know about Mary?"

"First, where is Hank Selmon? He hasn't been seen since he trained a winner for you last Sunday, and I want to know if anyone worked for you who was about five-foot-ten, 200 or 220 pounds, thick around the neck, maybe thirty-five years old and blond."

"Who are you working for?" Sarafin asked quietly.

"Myself, Mr. Sarafin. Just me. I've always been self-employed."

"Me, too. Always. Just a couple of entrepreneurs, right?" He handed the drink to me and motioned for me to try it. I did. It was warm and sweet and very smooth.

"Just a couple of enterprising boys," I said. "Listen, I just want to know about Mary Jarn. She died at my feet. I'd appreciate knowing more."

"Yes, Walter, so would I." A crooked streak that was supposed to be a smile broke across Sylvia Sarafin's brown face.

"Sylvia. Why don't you just leave Mr. Ace and me."

"No," she said. "It's not just *your* discussion, Walter."

Sarafin concentrated on me. "Do you have more questions?"

I was surprised at her moxie. Turkish entrepreneurs were not known to be easy on their women.

"Who kidnapped Mary Jarn several years ago? When did you fire Cyril Weber as one of your attorneys? and what makes your wife or you think that I have Hank Selmon's money?" I thought that I might as well hit him with the full load.

His jaw kept hardening. "Mr. Ace, I could have you tossed over the cliff right now and you'll never be missed."

"The police would miss me. They're waiting in Newport for me to show up." That was the last place I wanted to go. "You would miss me, too. I have some answers as well as some questions."

"We're glad you came, Mr. Ace, but we don't associate with your kind. We really don't."

"I'm the only kind you ever associated with, Sarafin. Just a couple of guys trying to get by in the world . . . entrepreneurs, remember?" He finished his sherry, slowly, thinking while the liquid disappeared. "The trophy collection, your shooting or the White Hunter?" I inquired.

"All mine, Ace," he said, no pretenses or sham left. "All mine and with one shot, even the buffalo."

Sylvia interrupted forcefully. "So now, Mr. Ace. I'm sure Henry will turn up. And if he doesn't we have no information that would help. We can't tell you about Mary. She's a closed book."

"Never," I said, "absolutely never. You *do* have information." I shifted back to Sarafin. "You know where everything is buried except for the $800,000, don't you Sarafin?"

He stiffened even more. His anger was unmistakable, even through the cool facade over his face. "If you wanted information, Mr. Ace, you have done everything possible not to get it. And since you are a professional finder— you see, I do know about you—then I must conclude you are not after information. What is it that you really want?"

"Wrong again, Sarafin. Information, what I need is information about Mary Jarn. And I want to know why you think I'm involved in a scheme to cheat you out of $800,000. And perhaps much more to come."

"It's just the money, right?"

"Wrong one more time. You don't get it, do you?—I really want to know. I'm not truly interested in you. I want to know why Mary Jarn was special; and where Hank Selmon is; and why I've been painted into a pro- verbial corner. Believe me, I don't mind stepping on the paint to get out. If I have to, I will."

He walked over to Sylvia and stood for a moment, silently. "Do you hear that, dear? Do you know why anyone would want to involve Mr. Ace in anything? Es- pecially in events we are ignorant about?" His voice be- came even more clipped, more foreign.

Sylvia did not move.

"If I knew anything about these things, Mr. Ace," Sar- afin said, "it seems to me you were foolish to tell me. Doesn't it simply place you in greater jeopardy?"

"Probably not. Because I have something else to tell— not to ask." My cynicism was returning. When you're in business, cynicism is a regenerating inventory. Sort of the last refuge of sanity. Instead of continuing to pump I laid my suspicions on the line. "I might as well tell you that I think someone is out to murder you and this someone is not the same person who killed Cyril Weber. It could be Henry Selmon and I think some new, very big trans- action is waiting for all the pieces to fall into line. It's all waiting there, just out of reach. It could be that I know you're the major domo in the deal, and it could be——."

In a gutteral half-whisper, Sarafin said, "Mr. Ace, you have spent your life involved in sickness and weakness and you have been used up in the gutters of society. That's where you belong. You are just bothering us now."

"But you're interested in what I have to say."

He shuffled. It was the first time he appeared to have any vulnerability. "I'm listening."

"Someone killed Cyril Weber who knew about an accident that occurred seven years ago in the California desert. Someone wants to even the score before the score card is lost and forgotten. You are the scorekeeper and ahead in points—at least for now. And someone who couldn't control a young and special girl decided that life was cheap, that young women are expendable, that a repeat of history was too dangerous."

Sylvia slumped painfully into the overstuffed red chair and laid her head back as if to faint.

"But," I continued, "you don't have all the marbles and you no longer control the situation. I think I may have all the pieces and faces together. A new shipment in the desert; but millions this time. Old alliances falling apart. Everything not quite in balance. One girl dead, one boy missing, one old piano player ready to burst. Don't worry. It's not meant to frighten—just to protect this body of mine." I was convincing myself.

"Anything else?"

"Yes. I don't have your money. Never did. Never knew it existed until one day ago. Your wife probably knows more than I do on that score. All I want is what I said. You can pollute the entire Imperial Valley with dope if *you* want. Give me what *I* want——" I hesitated "—— because I'll get it in any event. Trust me." Bravado seldom worked, but I had gone too far to stop.

"I think it's time to throw you out, Mr. Ace. Enough is quite enough."

"Walter," Sylvia interrupted. "Where *is* Hank?"

"Probably shooting himself up in some sleazy alley. How would I know?" His words slipped out of tight lips. His knuckles had turned white. "Get out, Mr. Ace. Enough."

He turned and pushed a buzzer and two very large young men appeared almost instantly.

"I'll show myself out, thank you. From here to my appointment with the police." I prayed that my story about the Newport Beach police waiting for me was believed. Sarafin wanted no involvement with the police. Like every businessman, he disliked government interference.

"By the way, Mr. Ace," Sarafin smiled and began to pour another sherry, "telling me about an imaginary assailant hardly succeeds"—he said *succeeds* as if his mouth were full of hot cotton—"in persuading me that you are simply a nice human being who made a long trip because you care so deeply. If you have nothing that I want, if all your suspicions about me are true, why is your life worth a dime? Why is your existence meaningful at all? In short, how long will you stay alive?"

It was as if I had been struck in the solar plexus. I had been so anxious to untangle myself from the web around my innocence that I protested too much and had gotten myself into the web's center. All horribly amateurish, all uncool. Since Sarafin was connected with Tony's story, I had to conclude *he* was after me, *Sylvia* was after me, *Selmon* was after me, *Sarafin* was after me, and the *police* would be after me, and I knew in my still-functioning deep intuition that there was at least someone or something yet unknown who needed me out of the way.

"The question is, Mr. Sarafin," I replied, "which one of us starts counting the hours first."

◆

As I drove slowly up the driveway to the street, Sylvia Sarafin waited by the gate, skin suddenly losing its color in the stabs of my headlights. I pulled onto the highway and shut the lights.

A minute later—"I'm alone," she said breathlessly, leaning in the passenger's window. "Can I come in?"

I flipped the locks. Slipping in she pushed the lighter, waited and shoved the red spiral to her cigarette. Leaning back, she inhaled slowly. Her face was exquisite in the red glow. Magazine-cover perfection.

"You change colors every five seconds, Mrs. Sarafin—or whoever you are."

"That's not true, Mr. Ace. A few mistakes. I've made a few mistakes. The colors have always been the same. Green for money and blue for sadness. It seemed so simple—Walter was my best shot—at a bad time in my life. So I took it. *That* was green. Since then, green and blue. Walter isn't just some international thief, you know. He's simply a go-between."

"A deadly arranger is more like it. Black would be his color. Why would you persist in lying about what he is?" I wanted to tell her that I knew the details of that night on the Mojave.

She sighed as if it were her last sigh. "We have a lot in common, you and me." She smelled like sweet fudge just cooling from the vat.

"We are not even remotely related spirits, Mrs. Sarafin."

"Sylvia."

"Mrs. Sarafin."

"All right, let it be Mrs. Sarafin."

"Just tell me about Mary," I said.

"She was a tramp. A tramp. An absolute tramp. Her

father didn't know she was alive. And like most kids who couldn't really connect, she drifted. She was crazy about Henry. And he about her. Then she became a pawn in Walter's game." Sylvia looked out into the dark. "She painted, you know. Past couple of years she became a good painter. Not commercial but First Trust Saving's art buyers got behind her. She paints as if her brush were dipped in tears. That's the only way I can describe it. But, God. She *was* a tramp."

"He kidnapped her to insure Henry's cooperation." She nodded.

I thought for a moment. "Anyone else's cooperation?"

"No one, not that I know."

"Have you seen Tony Antonnini's boy, William? I have a notion that Walter has him, too. Or he's involved in it." I presumed she knew what I meant.

"It's a nightmare," she said, paying no attention.

"Have you seen him?" I persisted.

"No, I haven't. I'm *trying* to help you. Really."

"Why are you telling me anything?"

"My god, you're dense!—I want out, of course. I want out of this nightmare. I'll help *you*. But get *me* out. I'll do anything."

She reached a slender hand toward me, but I pulled away and it dropped resignedly on the seat. For the first time I noticed that her fingers seemed to be assembled incorrectly.

"Tell me one thing. Did you know a blond fellow, the one I described in the house?" I asked.

"Yes. Henry hired him as my bodyguard when he was involved in all those dope deals in the past. Mary's former husband."

"Were his loyalties with you the whole time?"

"Well, he stopped working for us when I married Walter. But I think he was loyal. Why do you ask?"

"Because I think he was supposed to have called you—you or Sarafin—tonight. And I'm sure he hasn't."

"That's not so. I haven't seen Michael Jarn in years." Her hand pulled tensely back into a clutter in her lap.

"For god's sake, just tell me the truth; Michael is or was either working for you or your husband, and if not, then it's like I said, someone is after your husband—or you or me or all of us. There's no rhyme behind anything yet."

She shivered, dwelling for a moment on the possibilities. Her head raised, accentuating the length of her neck. I was creating a limited set of possibilities, not all of them. Sylvia was trying to get out all right, but with everything—all to herself, perhaps her and another player—or Sarafin had reached the point of ensuring an absolute result and was using his wife to use me and thereby reach the millions waiting for them in a deal that was very close to its closing day—all in one final conspiracy.

"I want out, Mr. Ace. I'll help you find anyone you want. I'll eat garbage if I have to."

There was a silence between us. The night had its sea mist swirling about the midnight lights. I didn't want to speculate anymore. There was a certainty in me that all speculations ended on my doorstep. In some way I was the catalyst; from a date before Mary Jarn's death, a shadow had been haunting me.

"Mrs. Sarafin," I said, "I'll see if I can help, but I'm at loose ends at the moment. Just call my name on the dial: Harvey A, by the numbers. The service will get through to me."

She leaned closer. I could see her breasts. The sheath was the only garment covering her tight, insistent body. She shivered again and grabbed me. "Will you help me?"

"I don't trust you. Not yet. Maybe sometime."

"Give me an answer," she insisted.

"No. You find William Antonnini for me. That's the

first step. Then we'll see. If you want to hire me—that's another matter."

"You're a cold son of a bitch, aren't you?" She drew away.

"I don't think I hold a candle to you, my dear. If I'm wrong, I'll apologize. Meanwhile, was Michael Jarn your lover? Are you in cahoots with Selmon, Sarafin, or somebody else? And what is that awful sweet smell in there?"

She opened the door and slid out. Her face smoldering, eyes glazed in anger. "When you walked in tonight I wanted to make love to you. Now I want you dead."

"Were you with Mary when she died?" I asked. Then I hurled question after question at her as she ran from the car, heels crunching on the gravel, sounding like grapenuts crunching between your molars. "Hey, Jarn is dead!" I hollered after her, finally. "I killed him."

Floodlights came on. People were running. I stuffed the Jag into gear and dug out. I wanted to lock a door to the world and tell her how Michael Jarn died and watch her face, and perhaps solve the mysteries.

The Jaguar grabbed at the highway as I thrust it into the night. I knew I couldn't go to the police. I would have to check the papers. I stopped and bought the San Diego paper and two local sheets.

In the *La Jolla Express* there was a two-column headline on the bottom right of the first page:

UNKNOWN ASSAILANT AT LARGE:
TWO MURDERS IN NEWPORT

Police suspect that two men, yet unidentified, were murdered in a drug-gang-related fight. Two half-pound sacks of cocaine were found in the plain Newport apartment located on Walnut Street. Police are now checking owner's and tenants' records to determine any connection but have no leads at present.

11

◆

Every muscle had gone on strike by the time I returned to the Sea View. Blue splotches spread over my right thigh. Michael Jarn had had a good time on me.

I found extra pillows and propped myself up on the bed and called Horse Blanket Billy. As the phone buzzed I began to count the strands of a tiny spider web just above the French doors that opened to the beach. Billy interrupted the reverie.

"I need help," I said.

He waited, knowing it meant trouble.

"I need you to stay on Walter Sarafin's tail and let me know when he leaves his place with his entourage."

"Am I getting mucho bucks for this?"

"Mucho. Just call the car-phone number when he makes his move." I explained the background and told him that I expected Sarafin to head north into the high desert. "And I would change my jacket if I were you. Try something sedate for this job . . . not that purple-yellow-and-green thing you've been wearing." For as long as I have known Billy he wore either the purple-yellow-and-green polyester job or the red-green-and-white job. In an undistinguished gambling career he had created a kind of personal distinction. A mark. An ugly mark, but you certainly knew when Billy was coming at you.

"Buy a blue gab jacket. Plain blue."

"I'm getting sick, Harvey. That color isn't right for me."

It was no use. I told him to watch himself, that the bad guys were really bad.

The light was probably still on when I slipped into painful sleep. In the caverns of my subconscious I heard an angry ocean. Waves slapped against the rocks and foamed out into clawing tentacles. They banked against my forehead and reached for my throat. My eyes were open; the pounding was still there. I rolled over and realized that I was awake.

The pounding made me sit up and then go to the door. Hank Selmon pointed an angry little .32 caliber pistol at my navel. He looked as bad as I felt. Jagged red lines occupied the corners of his eyes. He moved in a carefully controlled way. But the gun was level. I grunted.

His left hand waved me toward the other end of the room, and he shuffled in. His hands were extraordinarily large. In some Darwinian way, jockeys grew immense hands and feet. "I've been watching you," he rasped, "since you left the Sarafin place. It looked like you had great fun with Sylvia."

"I don't want any trouble, Hank. I've had my share the past couple of days."

"I'm not looking for trouble either, Ace. But *you* are a problem." His gun dipped slightly as I looked up. "I know you're after me. And I can't handle that right now."

"It's simple, I need to know about where you've been and what you're up to and why you're avoiding the entire world . . . but I'm not after you. Not like you think." I tried an easy smile. "Frankly, I suspected you were dead. I thought perhaps Sarafin or—never mind. Sit down. I have to get myself together. You look as bad as I feel. You've been on something, haven't you?"

He looked like a sick old man instead of a feisty 33-

year-old street bum with good hands and a clock in his head.

His voice came out in a savage whine. "What do you expect? Everything's screwed up. I'm going through the whole goddamn thing again. But this time I didn't want it. That's the joke. Last time I was itching for it and they took Mary. That was their insurance." He coughed out a miserable laugh.

"But not this time."

"Not this time." His body sighed, now beyond all weight limits, sagging at the belt buckle as if twenty years of beer had been added, instead of seven years of tension. "Not this time, Harvey. And you're part of it. Tony is out to get me because of Mary. He doesn't know the whole truth. Doesn't make any difference 'cause I'm not going to fool with you. I've gotta put you out of commission. There ain't any real choice. I've got it all figured out."

I told him that I was only looking for William, that my only connection with anything was to locate Tony's son. I kept talking. Somehow before he pulled the trigger I had to get close to him. His size and his semisedated condition made him vulnerable. I thought about the death of Michael Jarn. That's funny. I thought of it as a "death" not a "killing." The gyroscope of my morality had tilted.

"Henry, you're not going to shoot me. That's final . . . not unless you want me to kill *you* in the process. I'm not going to die in this stupid hotel room. It's as simple as that. No way. Wrong time. Wrong reason. Wrong person. I don't know what's going on in your head. But you ought to tell me. Maybe I can help. Let's just sit here, quietly, and talk it out."

"I can't trust you. I can't trust anyone. Everybody is angling for the double cross."

"And someone, like Walter Sarafin, is pulling the strings."

"Please, Harvey. Stay there. I'm not out yet. And I'm not too far gone." He bit the bottom of his lip. He was frightened. As much as I was.

"You can't squeeze that trigger, Selmon. There's no way. You haven't got it in you. Go ahead. Go on. . ." I urged, gently, thinking about how to move if his finger tightened on the trigger. "You've seen death before. It's a nothing item. You see it on the TV. Killing me has no meaning. Like everything, it's nothing . . . John Chancelor brings you today's killing and maiming, from Lebanon, from Indo-China, from your local city. . . . Death at the corner grocery. Death on Skid Row. Death in your bedroom. Death at the racetrack. Death———.' "

I rose. I was conscious of shouting and sweating at the same time. His gaze riveted on my face.

"Stop it. Christ, oh dear," he grimaced. "Stop it!"

I was on him. He realized it too late. The sagging gun hand came alive. I reached and crossed my hands. The pistol wrenched free and slid away, and I turned my back on him and picked it up. "Don't leave, Hank," I said grimly, "or I'll stuff you into a pillow." His whole being shrunk into a tiny convulsive state. My body was wet and clammy, juiced up by fear and hate or both. Selmon was feverish.

"Everyone's fucking me over," he said. "And you and Tony Antonnini are the lowest of the whole stinking bunch of them." He dropped himself onto the bed and began to shiver. "The two of you got together and cooked up Mary's kidnapping years ago," Selmon said. "You wanted me to bark when you snapped your fingers. You ate it up when he made me tell what a brain he was. He even wanted me to call him 'boss' and he would call me 'boy' like they did at the track. 'Hey, boy. C'mere, boy.' Then you worked up the whole switch routine with the money. You got all of the money, and I had to go begging Sarafin for handouts. Couldn't ride anymore—went up to 120 pounds. Too much booze. . . ." He rolled the bedspread into a coil around him. I didn't want him to stop. ". . . Too much coke. Sylvia was ready to hire someone to kill both of you. But you know who stopped her? Try that one. That tight-assed lady was ready to do it herself. Go ahead, guess who."

Nodding was enough. I urged him to finish. I wanted to explain my innocence but knew that I would have to wait. Twisting, he covered his mouth as he spoke. Somehow I felt as if he still held the gun. It was difficult to breathe easily.

"It was Walter Sarafin. He held her down. I couldn't. Sylvia and I were finished. I was only a means of getting her from rags to riches anyway." He paused. "She was somethin' though. For a guy like me from East L.A. she was hot stuff." Then he looked up, as if over the rim of imaginary spectacles. "You are one first-rate son of a bitch, Ace. A *picolo,* as we used to say . . . a real bastard."

I locked the door of the room from the inside. "Stay here. Quietly. Don't try to get out," I said. "I'll shoot you through one of the pillows before you get it open, and William will be a goner, like Mary."

In the bathroom I laid the gun on the brown formica and washed my face and hands. I scrubbed.

My eyes were at half mast. There were hundreds of tiny wrinkles that had grown into my cheeks and forehead over the last forty-eight hours.

I rejoined Selmon.

"What are you going to do to me?" Selmon asked.

"Let you go, probably."

"I'll pay you. More than Sarafin or Tony. Listen. We'll get William and then I'll finish the deal and you can have half my share." The idea grew on him and he brightened like a candle catching hold. "That's it. We'll get William and then you and I will do the deal!"

"You mean if you get the lion's share."

"Oh, don't worry about that," he said, feverishly encouraged. "I've worked it out perfectly this time. And I don't think they can hold William at all. I've got distribution all figured out."

"Maybe. Maybe you have. But there's someone else involved isn't there?"

"No one, You and Tony are it . . . and my former."

His face died down and the high shine on his eyes lowered. "Poor Mary. Goddammit—I could count on her . . . the only one. C'mon, Ace. You and I can handle the whole deal. I've got the contacts."

We compared discrepancies in Tony's recitation of past events and Selmon's recital. He began to laugh and cough.

"None of it makes any sense," he said, tiredly. "If I believe you."

"I think it's simple." I said. "Someone who can coordinate everything with almost complete impunity is setting up a very big payoff—but not until an old double cross is settled. I'm suspected of being part of that double cross, or I'm being used to make you and Tony and whoever else there may be believe I'm part of that resurrected deal. That old code-name Taurus deal."

"In all cases, you're dead." He almost smiled, his red eyes creasing up, fingers pulling at his right ear lobe. Still shivering he stared at me, incipient smile gone.

Five A.M. stillness hung in the room, and Selmon began to reminisce about "those days." He had lived on the streets. His father hardly ever left the Main Street Gym and the old boxing arenas. A tiny punk kid from the corners of Brooklyn and Soto in East L.A. had to be meaner and tougher and more talented than his peers. And Jack Selmon knew it. He tried to force the kid to fight, until he realized that he just wouldn't grow enough.

His uncle Tony, who dearly loved the horses, took the kid to the track, and he started exercising ponies at the L.A. Fairgrounds. He stayed mean. And difficult. And exciting. He had that dark electricity that tugged at the sensual zones of healthy women. Sylvia was older and shrewder than most. She joined in his defiance of the world when they were just kids. Until he began to sniff cocaine, and then she began to look for a way out.

"Nevertheless, she hired Jarn for that first deal. Tony told me that," I interrupted. "And he's the one who shot and killed that pilot during the exchange."

I opened the French doors. Pacific waves whispered distantly on the sand. It was just before dawn, at a time when the darkness was chilling. The yellow light of the room seemed to emit a stale sickness. I heard a toilet flush in a nearby room.

"Sylvia probably didn't know what kind of man she had hired," I said. "She didn't know what she was getting into. Listen, you have to take me to Bill; I can't let him rot away. I know you know his whereabouts. He had nothing to do with any of this."

"I can't take you to him. Are you crazy?" The old whine returned. "He gets loose again and stumbles right into the whole fucking mess again. . . . No dice, Ace! He's in protective custody. And I can't help him; besides, he's more dangerous than anyone. That kid is a little wacko. Tony never told you that, did he?"

I had enough. I stood him up and held him by the nape of the neck with one hand, and searched his body with the other. I found a Sucrets tin with white powder like granulated flour.

"Don't do that!"

"I'm reforming you, Hank," I said, and tossed the open tin over the balcony onto the dirt below. "Besides, the stuff is nonaddictive, right? You can handle it, right? All you get is a hard nose. And you've had that since you were fourteen. So what?"

"Shit, Ace. Shit! It would have been so easy to kill you."

"Easy for me. Not easy for you. Just remember. I've got the gun."

Dawn struck.

12

Sunsets are red and orange, and dawns are blue and green. If you don't like mornings, they're black and white. This morning was shades of grey.

"You're taking me back south again," I said. "Sarafin's house."

"Just turn the heat up."

The car was sweltering. But Selmon didn't stop shivering. He squeezed his arms against his chest.

"I'm used to booze hounds," I said, "not shivering fools hanging between oblivion and reality, like you."

"Just shut up and turn the heat up."

"It is," I replied.

There was a pause. And then, as if his brain all at once went into gear, he said, "You're one of those brainy guys like good old 'Uncle Tony' claims to be, aren't you?"

"Tell me what he claims," I insisted.

"S-S-Syracuse . . ." his teeth clattered. "Phi Beta Kappa, Syracuse. But you know all of that. You know everything about Tony. You've got the money and the two of you worked out this whole new transaction. A $100 million smackeroos. I know I'm right. Then, bang, bang—all of us get it in the head. You said so yourself. Killing don't bother you."

"The police want me for two killings, Hank. Cyril *and* that Jarn fellow."

He exhaled suddenly. "Oh, Christ, you killed Cyril, too? Oh, God, Cyril never hurt anyone. He just got stuck in the middle."

"Shut up. Just stop slobbering and sit there, quietly. . . . I didn't kill Weber."

"Bullshit!"

I reached across and smacked his cheek with the back of my fist. "I didn't kill him! I told you. Michael Jarn probably did."

His hands covered his face. Breathing came more deliberately. He could be a nasty little bugger, I thought. I remembered how he used to beat his mounts down the stretch.

"Can you stop this thing?" he sobbed. "I've got to take a leak. Don't worry. Tony's kid is OK."

I wheeled off the freeway to a bright Chevron station. I told Selmon to get out of the car after I did. He obeyed. We got the key and he went into the men's room while I stood outside. We were about two miles from the ocean on the side of a hill adjacent to one of the new housing projects that covered most of the hillsides from Newport to San Diego. The sea shimmered through the morning haze, spread out in deceitful repose. I put on my sunglasses.

Then I heard squealing from inside. I didn't bother pounding at the door but hollered for the attendant who ran for a key. Selmon was on cement, curled beneath the wash basin. His blood droppings were all around, like splotches of crushed liver. He held his wrist. I pulled him up. He was incredibly heavy.

"Not this time, Hank."

The wounds were not deadly. Bleeding for another slow mile clocking still wouldn't have done him in. I shoved his arms under running water and turned to the immobilized attendant. "Get me your medical kit. Let's wrap this."

A handful of Selmon's hair helped me force his head under the cold water. "Aw-right, aw-right," he blubbered. "S'nuff."

I held the upper part of his arm tightly, squeezing off most of the blood supply. After an amateurish wrapping of gauze and tape around Selmon's wrists, I gave the flustered, worried attendant five dollars and told him I was taking the "crazy little one" to the hospital.

"I've got your knife, your gun, and your number, Selmon. We had better not be on a wild-goose chase. William shows up or I'll shove you out while I've got this car at eighty. *N'est-ce pas?*"

"Aw-right. Doesn't make any difference anyway. My loss ain't no loss."

We unrolled the blazing carpet of the roadway. I drove carefully. The highway patrol always hid at the top of a freeway on ramp, and I kept my eyes on the rear-view mirror as I drove.

"Tell me what happened to Mary, Ace. Would you? I'm feeling shitty about her," he murmured, weakly. "It's all my fault."

"Someone forced a medication called Orinase into her. I also think she knew it and was about to write a note and hand it to me. I assume she got to the track with someone she trusted. I don't see how she could have been forced into that spot with the crowd around. It might have been Jarn or . . . whoever. She couldn't get to you so she gave me the next best person, Cyril Weber, your lawyer. I'll tell you something else. I think Sylvia Sarafin was with her, and that Sylvia may have directed the whole thing."

"It could only have been Walter and Sylvia."

"Or someone we don't know. Someone that, perhaps, Cyril Weber knew."

"Mary must have known everything. I just can't believe that Sylvia would be involved like this. She ain't no killer.

At least I didn't think so. She was just a girl who knew how to get ahead, you know, not from the streets like me, or like Antonnini pretends to be. In fact," he added, "I was crazy about her really. She took care of me in her way. Told me I was OK. Told me not to be afraid. She and Tony together kept telling me not to be afraid. Now the whole thing is starting over again. We've got another big load coming in, a very big shipment—very big—and this is all Walter's way of buying insurance, and Sylvia, too."

"But Mary found me," I reflected, "and now everyone is scurrying."

"They want an undivided take. No partners." He leaned back. "I feel nauseous, Ace. It's too much for my brain. I've lost too much blood."

"It's not the blood, Hank. It's the cocaine. You're still clammy. You must love that stuff. Stick your head between your legs. I haven't got time to take care of you."

He giggled crazily. "It ain't sex, so it must be love."

I was not convinced that the "they" in this question was simply Walter Sarafin, international wheeler-dealer. Even if it was, he wasn't running the day-to-day operations of his network, and if he wanted me killed, he could have had it done at any time. Now he was ready to receive a $100 million planeload of concentrated misery and oblivion somewhere in the Mojave, and a little man named Henry Selmon held the key to the timing of the connection.

"Why was Cyril Weber killed, Harvey?" Selmon asked. "I can't see any reason for it."

"He knew something, Hank, about Taurus probably. Or he found out something and tried to save Mary all by himself. Or he was part of the deal and he was ready to spill the whole deal."

"I'm getting sick," he mumbled with a helpless cry.

"Just hold on."

◆

Someone or several someones was following us.

I called Lew Mackin and explained I couldn't rescue a kidnapped boy from the Sarafin house, where I was certain he was being held, without help; that I was being followed already; I told him that I had smelled something peculiar, like ether, when I was at the Sarafin house the prior night and had decided that it was ether. "Stay put," he warned. "And stay out of it. Leave it to us. Do me a favor. Just let it be."

I declined. He started to tell me how a police bureaucracy functioned, how he had to call the La Jolla department, and the Sheriffs Department, until I interrupted and told him I would be at the Sarafin house in half an hour. If I had help, fine. If not, I used to consider him my friend and please, no roses. He told me I didn't know what I was doing. That accusation has always convinced me that whatever it was I was doing, it was the right thing to do. Experts never know the right thing to do. "Then I'm not responsible," was his parting shot.

The car behind me was close, openly following my lead. I reached over and grabbed Selmon. "Don't tell me that the Antonnini boy isn't there. They've drugged him, put him out of his head, and held him there. That little gang back there doesn't care that you're one of them. They'll put you out of your misery quicker than you can scream for help. So behave. You haven't been bleeding. Tell me all of the rest of it. . . ."

The car behind kept coming closer, without pretense, as Henry Selmon told me all the rest of it.

I pulled into the Sarafin driveway, onto the crunching gravel. Sarafin was caught in the flashes of early eastern sun. The sky-blue Buick behind me was now just feet away.

He was grinning. He had to be one of those people who was perpetually disappointed in his adversaries. He wanted a good game and more often than not got a lame try and shrug instead. "He's here," I said. "I want him and I don't want trouble."

Still smiling, all teeth and cheer, he said, "You could be an interesting person, Mr. Ace."

"Call the boys off. . . ." I tipped a finger at his goon squad. They were leaning on my car, also smiling. "Tell them to get their bodies off my car, and tell them to quit smiling. No smiles, you *capice?*"

"Such talk. My my." His hands were on his hips. He was deciding. Did he want to take me out now? . . . wait? . . . play the game? . . . Did he need the fuss? All of it churning around in that brain of his that cleaned out all the crumbs and left the raisins. I knew how he was thinking, what was going on in that handsome, rich, smiling, ruthless head.

His two guardians began to approach.

If I ran like crazy I might be able to save my ass.

I was counting on Lew.

A phone rang. It came from the phone in the Buick.

One of the uglies handed it to Walter. He spoke earnestly for a moment, hung up and began smiling again.

"I'm going through the house," I said.

"Please do. Hank can escort you. It's quite a lovely house. Hello there, Henry. *Ça va?*"

"Save the time and bring William Antonnini out and that will do it."

Just then a blue and white La Jolla police vehicle coasted down onto the driveway.

Two smiling uniforms got out and one approached Sarafin. He was young and not quite sure of himself and swaggered just a little. They had to know they were dealing with a very big person in their community. Sarafin gestured at the house. Both officers moved cautiously through the front door, nodding polite hellos to Sarafin's housekeeper.

The goons were caught between the police vehicle and mine. Each retreated quietly to the inside of the Buick.

I should have known. William had to have been moved as soon as they knew I was heading back in their direction.

The older policeman spoke to me. He looked down as he spoke, his sharp nose moving up and down like a gentle saddle ride. "Ain't no one in there, Mr. Ace, 'cept the maid. Not a soul."

"Mrs. Sarafin?"

"Doesn't look like anyone was there at all. And this Sarafin ain't just anybody, y'know. You ought to just go on along and meet us at the station and tell us about what went on in Newport. I think that's what we gotta do."

"I'm sure Lieutenant Mackin told you to cooperate with me. You know I didn't kill Weber and just happened onto him."

"Well, whyn't you just c'mon in and tell us about it. I hate to make a bother here. But——"

Sarafin smiled and waved as I drove off with a La Jolla police car as an escort.

It took three hours to get the story on tape, get Hank taken care of, two more phone calls to Lew to get me unstuck from the persistence of the interrogation. When I left the interior of the station, Hank Selmon was waiting. "I didn't have any place to go," he said.

13

◆

"I've just got to look at you," I told her. "I can never be sure that these kinds of moments will ever return. . . . You are god-awful beautiful. Every inch."

She was smooth and firm. Her breasts were raised, anticipating.

Sylvia Sarafin crawled across the sheets and put her mouth, very slowly, over mine. I felt drowned. Smothered. Too scary. I pulled away. That kind of close hit my rawest nerve ends. I struggled away. "Stand up again . . . for a while. I need to see it all again and get it perfect in my memory."

Exquisitely she unwound and stretched in the moonlight. The only light—blue light bathing her shoulders and breasts and the delicious lines of her waist. She posed as if realizing all at once how much she enjoyed it. I was lost in the moment, in time and space.

She had been waiting for me as I drove up. No speaking was necessary. In a predestined way we knew it would happen. She had followed me in, taken my hand and searched out the bedroom. She took a steaming bath as I lay waiting. As she stood caressing the night, drops of residual perspiration shone on her forehead. Tiny droplets reflecting the moonlight.

"I wanted to be with you since that first night," she

told me. "You make me shiver now when you touch me. I probably hate you."

"I'm sure of it. Hate is what makes us move," I said. "I'm not even in shock. Just pleasure. But I have a feeling . . ."

She curled into my arms and her strangely crooked fingers caressed my chest and arms. "Forget it," I whispered. "Forget everything."

I pulled her to me. Clutched her. She was willing. She had come to me to be loved—to be lost, to be made real. "I'm not real with him. I'm a bitch on a leash. I undress and stick my cunt in his face and he laughs, and I tell him I'm leaving and he laughs, and I tell him I want money and he laughs. So all I want is for you not to laugh and to make love to me, to all of me." She grasped me delicately, but with knowledge. I was conscious only of her hair falling in my face and her tongue in my mouth, and her breath. "You're trembling," she whispered.

"I've let go. Let go," I replied. I could not understand my shaking. I reached between her legs and held on. Breathless moans emerged from deep in her chest. Time stopped. My mind could see my hand and her hands in the dark, and her eyes. Wild eyes. Wanting eyes. "I want you inside of me. I want it inside of me," she said.

"Not yet." My voice was a crackled whisper, strange to me. I remembered trying to feel like this—being afraid—when I was married and when intimacy seemed so easy but was actually so difficult and so fearful.

She stroked me with excitement and I heard myself sigh with something more than pleasure. I couldn't open my eyes. She whispered, "Come. Come."

"No. Hold on. I want to hold on."

Her mouth moved down and I was engulfed and couldn't move, and held everything. Pulling away suddenly, she pushed my penis into her and we rolled around on my back and then on hers, the sheets entangled into us until all at once from a great depth I heard a laugh. A throaty laugh. And I laughed myself and it came roaring out. Blasting unrestrained and she screamed, "Come! Come on. Come on!"

And I did and her body quivered. Receiving me. All of me. And I pumped and she pumped and she squirmed involuntarily. Her head tilted backward and shook from side to side. She cried, my mouth involved in her tears. I was in sudden despair and she was unthinking, eyes staring, breath straining through her throat. "I don't want to stop. Please. Hold me. Come again. We can't stop."

I held her, rolling back and forth, like holding a lost child. It was over. Emptiness overtook me. Crying loneliness. Back to the same place in existence. Returning home to what always was. Quiet, forlorn—childlike in age and childlike in depravity. Holding Sylvia was like holding the moment that made me alone. She said, "I don't want it over—you. You stranger. You fool. You cheat." I was none of those and all of those, still in the midst of the only kind of intimacy that was not intimate. I was all of her accusations and desires, having never been in the final act of intimacy—defenseless and utterly, miserably dependent. Intimacy, I knew, was never known by healthy bodies. It was a state of being achieved by the crippled and lame, and was persistently painful and humiliating. I would never be dependent—and humiliated. Yet I was. Then, that minute. I felt as if I had suffered humiliation at her bequest. And she was not lost in her fear. She cried, sobbing deeply.

Glassy-eyed, almost frenzied, she told me about Walter Sarafin and Henry and Anthony Antonnini. She told me about a dead child, hers and Henry's. "God, how I wanted to die when she died." And she told me about using dope to make the pain disappear and how Henry seemed to succeed, but how she needed more and found and used Walter, and how he used her. Abused her. That was it.

She used him to deaden the pain and he used her to create pain, twisting her fingers while they fornicated, holding a hand over her mouth and twisting her fingers until the fingers cracked like dry pencils, and humming balefully until he heard the cracks. Her fingers would be bound for weeks and she would keep her hands bound long after the fingers had healed.

"That smell," I said, "like ether. When I was in your house."

"He used it on William."

"And what else?"

"And dope . . . William believed. Walter made a believer out of him. Like he made out of me after my baby died. I don't want to feel like that ever again."

"A long time ago?"

"Ages."

Once again silence fell. Like the first time. I lay on my back strangely grateful yet sorry that I had been involved in these last minutes.

"I want out," she said finally. "Somehow, I've got to get out of this."

"I'm not sure you want out."

"I'm telling you. I *need* out."

"All you need to do is walk. Walk out."

"With what? Good breasts aren't enough. I need the money."

"What money?" knowing what she meant.

"I want the money you have. The $800,000. Or whatever Anthony has salted away for you. I want that money and I want this new shipment. Whatever it is. I know it's coming. Somebody is setting it up very carefully—and it's not anybody in this cast of characters. Somebody, somewhere, is pulling the strings. And you're his lackey. Not Walter, not Tony, not anyone. Everyone listens."

"Like E. F. Hutton."

"I've got to get to the money. I've got to. . . ."

"You are a small fish in a big pond, Sylvia." Her first named sounded strange and distant when it came out. "Even if your suspicions were true, you don't have the means."

She rolled over onto me, and whispered, her face too wildly beautiful and tormented to trust. "I feel better now. We made love beautifully. Superb would be the word. Kids don't know."

Something wasn't right. Same old feeling.

"Are you going to help me, old Ace? Grey Ace. Lover Ace."

"Probably not."

"We can do whatever you want. I won't go back. I'll stay here. I'll hide . . . but you've got to give me the money." She kissed me, slowly. All at once I felt exhaustion grab her. She buried her face into my neck. Her legs drifted between mine. "I'm so tired."

"Sleep, lady. Sleep it off. Daytime makes everything better. More real."

Her voice slid from her throat. "I may have to kill you, Ace, unless I get the money . . ." she laughed. "But there's no hurry. Is there? You'll help me."

I pushed her away as she drifted into sleep, half-dreams, all-vengeance.

Later, just before dawn, after staring at her for hours, I watched her shower and dress wordlessly. All beautiful and elegant again, she smiled and reached into her bag.

"It's gone," I said, showing her the small .32 caliber she had hid in it.

"If *I* don't get the money, *you* never will," she said, all straight and clear-minded again, all hard and distant again.

"Why do you presume I still have it? Assuming anything you say is correct?"

"Money always rises. Harvey. Like cream. Sooner or later it rises and you can see it, clearly. So far, no cream."

She held up her hands. "Believe me, Ace. These fingers are my witnesses. Until Mary came to you, I was never sure about the money. Now I am . . . I'll do anything."

She was gone.

I fingered her address book. Soon I would know the secrets of Mary Jarn.

And suddenly I felt hunted.

14

"He was found wandering on the highway, that same afternoon."

"Near Sarafin's?"

"Near enough. About six miles down the Coast Highway, north of Laguna Canyon Road. Still slightly under the influence; probably Demerol. Now you can go home and get out of the finding business. It's all over."

"I'm not in the business, Lew. This was for Tony."

"Well, it's over," he repeated, his voice cracking over the airwaves from L.A. to my car phone. "So go home and quit all this."

"Damn! That drives me crazy. Do I tell you what to do?"

"All the time. Harvey, for chrissake, trust me on this one."

"What about arresting Sarafin? What about Sylvia? She's just an addict with a dream about how to get out of her mess."

"What about minding your own business? Let the police do their job. I'm telling you."

I had put Henry Selmon to bed. He had told me the details of Tony's plan. "If Walter's filly Ring Girl is scratched on Friday, that means it's on. Forty-eight hours later a planeload, maybe worth a hundred million 'street' . . . lands near the southwestern edge of Death Valley. Same as last time. A hundred million. A hundred mil. Hear?"

As I left I thought how seedy he had become. From the top of the world to cold dirty cement floor under a washbasin in a smelly gas station lavatory.

———————◆———————

William Antonnini turned abruptly as I entered his room. His thick young torso stiffened. I felt controlled mayhem hiding behind his darkly intense, almost hateful glare. Every emotional sinew of the young man was directed at me.

But Tony smiled from ear to ear, his entire face crinkling up like a weathered bedsheet. "Everything's OK now!"

"You gotta be kidding," I said. "Mary Jarn's dead. No one has redeemed her. That's what she wanted from me. And I know, well . . ." I looked at William, still staring at me. "Well, Henry certainly can tell stories."

"It's all over, Harvey. My worries are over. Can't you see?"

"Your worries are just beginning, Anthony."

Tony's smile sunk like a bowling ball dumped in water. "You're going now, Harv. Right? Bill's got to get some rest. I appreciate everything you did, but it's over. Llewelyn Mackin will be here in the morning to take another statement."

"They didn't get one yet?"

"Yeah, yeah. They got one. Spent three hours. But it's over. Harvey. Over." His voice rasped with irritation.

"Everyone keeps telling me that." I turned to William. "You look like hell, kid. You ought to cough it out.

Because whatever it is ıt sure is sticking in your craw. There's somethig you have to tell me, isn't there? Something you haven't come up with yet."

"There's nothing to say."

"That's it?"

He didn't reply. Slicing me up as if with deadly laser beams.

"Why me?" I said to his silent face as I left.

"Why not?"

Tony followed me to the door. "I think they must've done a number on him." He looked up and seemed suddenly bent and tired. He was thinner than I remembered, just since I saw him a few days ago. "My boy isn't usually like this."

"From what I can tell, he *is* usually like this. Hank says he thinks something is wrong with him."

"That's crap, Harv. We know each other a long time. Wouldn't I tell you if I had problems with my own son? Wouldn't I say something?"

I supposed he would and then told him that I thought the police had a lock on his dates and times. I said, "Don't do it, Tony. If Lew doesn't stop it, I'll stop it. One way or another. You don't need it. It's too crazy. You've got your kid back. You're out of it."

He planted himself, like an old fighter, weaving slightly. It suddenly struck me that he was very, very sick. "No one knows. I'm telling you, no one knows anything, except you. Anyway, it ain't so easy to get out, Harv. It ain't so easy."

15

◆

Llewelyn Mackin was very close to retirement. It had gotten to the point where the thought of the last day of his police career occupied his mind more than was safe for a cop. He knew it. Though he tried to maintain a decent level of concentration, the best he could muster was a facade—a reflective facade. He substituted his reputation in place of decisions and analytical thought processes. None of his lapses had made a difference, as yet. He knew he was tired. He kept thinking, "burn out." An easy phrase—but correct.

When he left his apartment each morning he counted the days he had left. Not on a calendar, but in his head. Standing at the front door he would gaze carefully into each corner of the room, at the elongated lamp shade tilted drunkenly toward the wall, at the threads on the arms on the tweed couch, at the melmac remaining on the yellow formica dining room table, and he would try to pull his belt over his belly and would say, one day less . . . 102 days left.

All the years alone accumulated into one lonely pattern of habits. And the past few years the habits were less than tidy. He worried as to whether or not marriage would really work for him, whether or not freedom from structure would work, whether a civilian's view of life would be sufficient to fill all his corners. Nothing was orderly anymore, especially when she wasn't around. Orderliness was a trait of an alert mind. He decided that when he was 25. No ends undone. The world picked up after Einstein, he thought, so his existence was kept neat. He could not have functioned if the melmac wasn't washed and dried after every meal. If Einstein had to do his own dishes, the properties of light and energy might still be seeking a cohesive theory.

When his last day came, it would be a new beginning. The army was a beginning, the LAPD was a beginning, and leaving the LAPD was a beginning. He had always been employed, drawing a check and reporting to a superior. He could not conceive how a human being could manage without reporting to an overlord or without having a known amount of money each month to parcel out to creditors. And if he had known a long time ago that more than three beginnings in life were necessary, he would have taken to drink.

So he went to work at the same time each day and kept a low profile and made suggestions out of habit and was pleased when he came home and found everything orderly and Julia waiting with a sweet smile on her lips inviting a serene future.

And he knew me very well. I had been a hotshot, the kind that burns out more quickly, who is more readily overcome by events and sometimes ends up as a suicide. Boundaries were forgotten, like kids playing ball on a too small sandlot. I remembered my last conversation with Lew before I quit the army. He said that he felt as if he were standing between a dark room and a light room, and that his feet were glued to that spot. He was captured in perplexed indecision. I also remembered that I replied, "One day you won't wait for the action anymore, Lew. You'll make it happen. Just like I try to do."

When I finally arrived home, there was a call waiting

for me. I didn't bother to return it. After all, it was all over. I was out of it. William was home.

I reached for the phone. Company would be nice. Elizabeth's voice sounded blurred with sleep, or something. After two minutes of trying to rouse her, I told her my door would be open, then shut the lights and pondered the night, wondering if I could handle someone being there, waiting for me everyday, every evening when I came home.

16

◆

He wore a grey hooded sweat jacket and pants and dusty tennis shoes, and carried a finely wrought rifle with a telescopic sight that made night into day and morning fog into noon sunlit clarity.

He was a mile or so from the Venice pier where isolated surf fishermen sat in fetal positions on aluminum chairs sunk deeply into the damp gray sand. On the pier more fishermen huddled beneath their blankets and shawls and spoke to one another in warm comradeship, holding steaming mugs of hot coffee, speaking between fog-horn blasts every thirty seconds.

A coterie of elderly women habituées wearing their habitual strawhats over flannel hoods and half torn blankets squatted near their pails at the end of the pier. The ladies were white. But the men were Greek and Asian and Mexican and Black, and knew one another from years of sitting at the same station. They caught smelt and sea bass, calico and herring, and the occasional bonita which were wonderful fighters. Mackerels were fun, too, but you couldn't eat them unless you were very hungry. They all caught pink starfish and sold them to the Japanese restaurants on the west side of town. Surf fishermen sat alone and brooded, as did the agile man with the rifle, hidden from sight by the sand dunes and fog. The surf was heavy and noisy. Isolated, empty lifeguard stations poked into the dimness for miles in each direction from the pier.

The rifle bearer was familiar with the habits of beach-front apartment and condo dwellers along that stretch. One lady arose at dawn each morning and, cold or bright, rain or shine, stepped outside and hummed to a vigorous set of calisthenics, pendulous bosoms clapping about but not interfering with the rhythm and regularity of her regimen.

This morning, he thought, was perfect. Good visibility. The heavy air would deaden the sound. He could break down the rifle and head for home, and that would be that. Perspiration secreted in a thin line along his upper lip like viral shingles. He didn't feel differently, but the droplets were always there. It had something to do with his childhood. He had read enough of those new psychology books to know that it all came from his childhood—but it didn't matter. Everything was here and now, as if childhood never existed. He was glad he was educated. It made one very calculating. He wasn't killing. He was eliminating. It had to be done.

He never thought about missing—just getting the job done. This job was difficult. The subject was unpredictable. It fascinated him. He was either not where he was supposed to be or he was behind a stud, obscured by a drape, sitting at the fireplace protected by brick—as if he had a sensitizing device in his cervical cord. Consistent people were dull. Consistently inconsistent people were banal, unworthy targets. But inconsistently inconsistent people were fascinating.

He moved closer to the subject's house, crawling patiently over the antarctic stillness. There was more than one person stirring. He had come back to the lonely space just before dawn. Being away too long did not change his luck. Harvey Ace was almost always alone, as now. The gunman was a hundred yards from his target's great windowed door. Pushing his body into the sand, he raised a sand shelf in front of him.

His hands, as if separate from the rest of him, dusted themselves off and then pulled a white napkin from beneath his sweatshirt and unfolded it and opened it neatly over the shelf. He cradled his rifle on the napkin along with his chin. He wiggled and made himself quite comfortable and then glued his eye to the sight and sighed, feeling a coolness along the ridge of his upper lip. He would observe for a while. It was fun.

17

◆

In the distance, the sea thundered like clouds nudging one another. At the end of a tunnel, I heard a bell calling me. I could see a hand reach into a spotlight, pick up the bell, shake it, then disappear. I saw Mary Jarn's white, dirtied face. Then the bell rang again, agitated. Ringing angrily. I hated shrill noises.

Elizabeth stirred and pushed her body closer to mine.

"H'lo." I cleared my thoughts. It was Walter Sarafin. "H'lo—yeah, I know who it is——Yeah, why so early? It's not even five."

"I prefer the solitude of these hours, Mr. Ace."

"Cut out the bullshit. Why are you bothering me?"

Elizabeth's hands crawled around my chest and she said, "Umm."

"I need to talk to you. And make arrangements to do so," he said slowly, as if to a child.

"That's what phones are for," I said.

"Mr. Ace. I think I can appreciate your belligerence, but I simply need some time with you. I do not discuss my affairs on the phone. Can you make it Friday? This coming Friday. It's Thursday morning."

"I know when and what it is," I snapped, still being pulled by my disturbed sleep. "But I'm not sure I want to meet with you unless I get some cooperation, too."

"I'm willing to try to help you. I couldn't talk at our

last meeting. How about the fourth race at my box Friday afternoon. I'll make a point of being alone." The receiver suddenly began to hum. Dammit! No one ever says good-bye. "Everyone hangs up on me!" I screamed.

"Who's calling at this crazy hour?" Elizabeth asked.

"Just a man." I rolled toward her and palmed her butt and dragged her into the curve of my body. "Just a man called Sarafin."

She stiffened. "Sarafin?"

Unfortunately, the time had come to interrupt my rest and recreation and get things straight with Elizabeth. I would have preferred waiting till mid-morning.

"Yes, Elizabeth—Sarafin. I think you ought to tell me about him . . . everything."

Her legs were like four-by-fours. Her buttocks tightened and she drew away. God, I thought, I'll never get close to another woman again. When she turns off, it's like holding dry ice—biting and burning your skin and freezing your insides. My heart frosted over but my head came alive. I wanted to hear every nuance in her voice and feel every silence.

"Harvey, I really don't know anything about him. He just brings back memories. Just a bad time in my life. That's all." Her voice was too contrived.

"How long were you married to Michael Jarn?"

She exhaled and sunk her head into the pillow. "I didn't know you knew about that. Oh, so what. . . . So what. You've got to know. You certainly know hard questions and soft spots . . . I was married to him all right." She shivered. Her voice grew quiet. "I was married to him six months. I guess I knew what he was at the start, but couldn't face it. You know? . . ." She stared blandly.

"He was tan and blond with great green eyes. But the minute he got control he was like a cruel child. He played physical games with you—he worked for Walter Sarafin. That's how I got to know Sarafin. But Sarafin didn't trust him either. Michael was so unpredictable that no one could do anything with him. I know he had another girl somewhere. I couldn't have satisfied him. We didn't have anything going after a while. And he used to disappear. You know, the same old eternal triangle bit. But I never could figure out who it was. Either she was a lunatic or she managed to keep control." She turned. "Why do you want to know about *these* people?"

"Well, Elizabeth," I said, slowly, "somehow, years ago, all of *these* people became a part of my life. I stopped being involved with anyone, really involved, that is, many years ago. Which is not important now. But way back then—everyone got the mistaken notion that I was part of something. Which I wasn't. I'm trying to get out of something I wasn't in. So I need to know as much as I can."

"None of it makes any sense, Harvey."

"I know, Elizabeth. It doesn't make any sense that you happen to be in my bed and just happened to be married to someone who was part of all of it. I wonder what other coincidences I'll turn up. I'm afraid to let myself fall into more than a medium-like condition with you."

"And love?"

"I'm not ready for that."

She turned her head, tossing her thick hair over my shoulder. "There are no more coincidences. And I don't think I want to know anything about what happened in your past—I've got my own life to live."

Sarafin had business ventures all over, she told me. Michael had taken trips for him to a trucking company in Phoenix, a paper bag distributorship in San Diego, a flower-growing business near Santa Cruz, tucked between hills of artichokes and oak trees and peach trees and cherry trees. "Finally, I left Michael and got a job at the steward's office. That's where we met. I suppose you can remember that."

I didn't answer and pulled the pillow into the crux of my arm.

"Harvey, I want to make love. I don't want to talk anymore. I don't want you to play Henry Higgens."

"It's all age, my dear. Great wisdom, old bones, and fear."

"And never love?" She reached between my legs and caressed me, and her mouth covered mine in moist warmth and I fell willingly into her desire as if into an abyss. Her lips moved steadily down my body. Everything caressed everything. Blue dawn touched the mist around us. Her mouth closed around me. My head tilted up. Then I was inside her. Eyes closed. Dark. Forgetting everything.

After we arose, I made notes, adding information on Sarafin and Michael Jarn. Then I stood for a long time under a steaming shower. When I was done I draped myself and went to the kitchen to put up coffee. I looked out toward the ocean. Fog diminished color. The world was faded. I reached to open the window.

"Elizabeth?" I called. "Do you——?"

It hit me before I finished.

II

18

━━━◆━━━

When all is said and done, the state of being is only a rental of time. The moment before birth and the moment after death are not known. We are suspended between the void times, hanging by a chance blend of character, brains, genes, and accidents of fate. I encountered another void moment: recollection of where I had been for several hours prior to being struck by a bullet.

Lew Mackin leaned close and told my ear that I wasn't dead and to quit hoking it up. Memory cells banged together at imprecise angles like sick protons. As the voice in my ear became more insistent, recollections of my father tripped in my head. He was standing in a narrow hallway pointing at my mother who I couldn't see. I didn't like the feeling that my father's image gave to me. He was shaking his head and I knew that my mother was nodding disapproval.

Lew's presence took over.

"Am I alive?"

"If this is living, then you're doing it," he replied.

"I saw my father a minute ago . . . but not my mother."

"You're entitled. You had a very close one, Harv. Very goddamn close."

A tinge of antiseptic permeated the softly circulating air. The blinds were half-open. Light fell joyfully around the room. My eyes worked. They focused on Llewelyn Mackin.

"It's funny seeing my dad standing in the hall like that." Hot Q-tips seemed to have been shoved around my gums. "C'n hardly talk." A cold seltzer. That's what I wanted.

"Smack your lips. Keep doing it. Like chewing."

I did it. "Now I know that I'm not dead. My head is busting. Brother . . . can I have some cold water?" I closed my eyes and started to press my fingers against one of my temples and jerked back. "Ow . . . that must be the spot."

"That's the place."

"You ever see your father in a fog like that? Don't know why it should be."

I heard a voice say, ". . . come out of it yet?"

Mack said, "Yeah, he's out of it. And talking. More than usual."

"Good," the other voice said. "I'll be back in a few minutes. Get him to drink some water."

I guzzled the luscious cold liquid. "What happened to me, Mack?"

"You were right. Someone is upset with you. I told you to stay out of it. Tried to blow your head into tiny pieces. In fact, he would have except that the bullet clipped the very edge of the window frame and veered off slightly. It grazed the right temple area above the ear and died in the wall two-and-a-half inches over the fireplace. There was a four- or five-degree angle to the trajectory . . . that meant——."

"OK. OK. Cut the Dick Tracy stuff. First talk to me."

"Have more water." He poked the bent straw at me again.

"Oh God, that's good." Instant recovery. "More."

"You're a lucky sonofabitch. It was so close this time, Harvey, that I called Kim. I expect her to call back anytime."

"You shouldn't have. She's got her own problems. You know how it is with lost young women."

A rush of anticipation rose in me. I hadn't spoken to Kim in a few weeks. I took another sip of water.

"Tell me more, Lew. Go slowly. Then I'll exchange as much as I can."

"No. No. We are not playing that game, Harv. This time it's no runaway kid. For all intents and purposes, you were assassinated four hours ago. You have to tell me everything."

Speaking evenly, almost whispering, I said, "All right, just tell me what *you* know."

Llewelyn Mackin sighed and pulled up a chair. He told me how he had envisioned the killer's actions before he cranked off his shot. The angle proved he was lying in wait on the damp beach. No one heard the shot fired. But one neighbor, Mrs. Gaffey, heard the window tear apart and the crashing of glass. She also heard Elizabeth start to scream, so she went inside and closed her door and decided not to exercise but to take a warm shower.

Elizabeth called the operator, and the police arrived about 20 minutes after the incident. She didn't touch me at first, believing I was dead, but I groaned shortly before the paramedics arrived and she sat on the kitchen floor and held my head, blood on her hands.

"The report was in my division when I got to the office," Mackin said. "It was you—so I volunteered."

What he didn't tell me until much later was that the report also was linked to an expected shipment of narcotics directed to one major dealer; that suspects in the warehousing scheme included Sylvia Sarafin, Hank Selmon, and a mystery man yet to be identified but who was likely a longtime friend or associate of Hank Selmon.

He told me that nothing in the police file revealed a reason for the attempt on my life except reports that I was associated with all the players and there appeared to be a possible double-deal somewhere in the cards. The police had informants in the middle of most transactions, I thought. At least they had enough informants on the street to know that a big dope deal was in the making.

"All we really know," he continued, "is that Mary Jarn died reaching out to you. Both Elizabeth and Mary were married to the man you killed in Newport. And he worked for Walter Sarafin. Sarafin's never been caught at anything and he pals around with rich Turkish diplomats. Not Colombian or Bolivian. Turkish. Now we have to deal with friggen Turks. His reputation is that he does everything as gently as possible, but he gets it done. We have a photograph of him with a retired Turkish general who lives like the King of Siam. All those connections boil down to Harvey Ace . . . and there it gets all fuzzy. Maybe this elusive Ace fellow is the mystery man . . . maybe?"

"Not bad. But there have got to be more pieces. *You* know——."

"But aren't telling——"

"Right. I guess I can't ask for more from my one and only best friend. . . ." I caught his eyes squarely. His gaze dropped away. There really was more; a lot more, I thought. "Listen, help me up. What happened to Elizabeth, anyway?"

He pressed his thumb into a white button on the bed post and my head rose.

"She's in the foyer on this floor. Waiting. It appears to me like she might be an interesting lady. Little bit young, but what the hell. She's pretty."

"No plans, Mac. I don't think I could take on a real relationship now. It's best for . . ." I hesitated, "*mature* fellows like us to stay away from involvements."

"But the harder you try, the worse it gets."

"Seems like it."

I wanted to change the subject, but Lew came back to

the puzzle. "It's your turn, Harv. You've got to tell me
what you know. Everything almost connects."

"Llewelyn, my friend, I can tell you that I didn't know
the girl, am not involved in dope dealing, and that I killed
one of the men found in that pink apartment house in
Newport in absolute self-defense, which you know, and
that I still have a huge headache."

A nurse entered briskly. "Mr. Ace, there's a young lady
waiting——"

"Tell her to wait," Mackin said, firmly. Then he said,
"You shouldn't be here. You should be in jail or dead.
You know lots more. You've got to play fair. I *need* the
information."

"Maybe there's more—but it's just guesswork. That's
all I can say, so take me away."

He was silent. There wasn't much more, so far as I
knew. But I also knew somehow that Mackin was lying,
and it hurt. His belly rose and set rhythmically. Breathing
through his mouth made him wheeze. "I don't need to
'investigate' anymore, Harvey. I know what I need to
know."

"I'm sure of it, Lew." There was silence. Breaking the
sudden awkwardness between us was difficult. "Listen,
in a few months, you can just tell the world to fuck off."

A tilted grin traveled across his round face. "Oh, God
almighty, will that be nice. Retirement. I can throw away
the Maalox. Six decades of life and I'm beginning to think
seriously about girls."

"And I'm in my eighth menopause and still can't get
girls off my mind. Listen, are you going to take me to
jail?"

He stood up. "You are going to be an informant for
us, Harvey, willing or unwilling. If it's willing," he said,
all smiles now gone, "you have no problem about being
involved. If it's not willing—then, Harvey, you're one of
the suspects in the drug deal and we take it as it comes.

We'll get the whole bunch. But we would like to avoid killing everyone in the process. Not because of morals, mind you—but because we don't like getting shot at during those final scenes either. And if we get the whole local network alive, we make the headlines. Good for the brass. They love that stuff."

He wheezed softly as he rested first on one wide foot then the other. The room weaved gently as I tried to raise myself higher. I remembered that I had to be at the track Friday afternoon. I didn't want Lew to interfere. Threads might ravel into some meaningful pattern.

"Harvey. This will be a big bust for me. I can get out with my armor still shining. Right now, even if I wanted a hot assignment, I wouldn't get it. Whadaya say?"

"Can't do it, Mac. If I play your game and follow your rules, I might not get my assassin before he gets me. I've got to do whatever is necessary my way, or my expert opinion is that I'm a dead duck. And frankly, something tells me to keep my mouth shut."

"I want to get the maniac who is after you, Harv. He won't miss next time. The scene will not be pretty when it all comes together. I won't bust you. I'll use you. Think about it."

"I'll be at the last scene—alive," I answered.

———————◆———————

Elizabeth sat on the bed while a hospital resident explained how lucky I was. He was releasing me tomorrow morning. I disagreed, and he told me no dice, one night's rest, otherwise I would be a candidate for fainting spells and blackouts. Concussions were like that. He started to lecture and I cut him off and asked him to leave. His thick black hair made me feel old and tired. He smiled on the way out and wagged his finger.

Elizabeth looked a trifle bleary. Then Kim called, and a resigned sigh rose from her breast, and she left.

"Hiya, luv," I said airily.

"How you doin', pop?" Her voice made me perk up. It had an adolescent melody to it, although she was quite grown.

"I'm doin' fine. Got hung up on someone's BB gun, though."

"Not according to Lew, pop."

"Lew? Now it's Lew. What happened to 'Uncle Lew'?"

"Tell me really, dad, how are you doing? Lew said you almost bought it and he was frightened. That's not like him, you know."

"Your voice sounds scolding."

"It probably is."

"Uncle Lew is ready to retire. He wants to live through the next few months in one piece, but he asked for this case. And he doesn't like it. Too much cops and robbers for him."

"Is the whole thing serious?"

"Enough, Kimmy. I'm fine. Uncle Lew will look after me. I want to know how the exams are going at school. How's your love life? How's that . . . you know, that Jonathan creep? Give me the lowdown." My head split in the forehead and the room went fuzzy. I tried to breathe evenly. That punk full-head-of-black-hair doctor was right. You *can* get dizzy.

I heard Kim say, ". . . and so one more oral exam and a redraft of the last 20 pages of the thesis and I hope that's it. I'm tired. It's hot as pure sin here. Humid and miserable."

"Suppose I sent you a ticket to visit me right after the last exam. Take a week off from the job. All of my business will be done by then, and we can spend a week doing nothing but running on the beach and playing volleyball."

"I can't just pick up. I've worked too hard. This new

job has promise. You get the bills, don't you want them to stop?"

"Oh, c'mon, Kim. Make it just a week. Even a few days. . . ." My throat dried up.

"Pop, I would," her voice lowered, "but I've got promises to keep. . . . Listen. I'll come out in the fall. I've got to keep at it. Lotsa competition here. . . . Are you feeling OK?"

"Yeah. Feeling good. A little misty and much more cynical and a big headache."

"You ought to settle for the quiet life."

"No lectures."

"OK . . . I love you, pop. Keep your head on. I was hoping you were through with that kind of life."

Her reference to "that kind of life" made me angry. "I'm retired, Kim, I live a quiet life. I don't have 'that kind of life' anymore. Anyway, it's my business. Let's keep it that way."

"I'm sorry. I'll call soon."

"I hope so."

She was going to hang up and I wanted her just to stay on the phone. I wanted to say I love you but said, "OK, kid. Talk to you. Thanks for the call." The minute I hung up, I wanted her back.

19

◆

I was going to get Mary Jarn out of my mind once and for all. I told Elizabeth to get my car. She balked and complained of tiredness. I saw my choices as sitting tight and waiting for Mackin to apprehend my thwarted assassin, running into hiding—Acapulco, Lake Louise or a solitary High Sierra cabin—or venturing out. The choices were not good, and my training made me respond without too much reflection. My problem was that I was not sure that I trusted anyone in the scenario.

When Elizabeth was gone, I gingerly rolled myself out of bed. One leg over the side, then the other, then roll upright and turn. That's the way; then you alight, facing the bed and holding on. Just as I made it up the same nurse appeared.

"There's a man——*say!* What do you think you're doing?" She was about forty and not bad. Her dusty brown hair curled in front of her cap and framed a ruddy, outdoors face.

"Just gettin' going," I said.

"Get your wounded ass back in that bed, mister, or I'll call the resident."

"It's not my ass that's wounded, nurse. I wish it was. You can tell anyone you like. Won't make a difference." I let go of the bed and stood straight. She came toward me, resignedly.

"All right, I've seen that macho look on male faces before. I'm not big enough to stop you and I really don't like that twerp of a resident we have on this service." She held me on the chest and back with firm, interesting hands. The circulation got going. "Here, tilt your head down and I'll push on your neck at the same time. Then we'll bend slowly forward and see how you do. Ought to get the blood back behind your eyeballs."

"OK. Slow now."

We tried it. No ill effects. Then I sat heavily on the green naugahyde chair and looked out the window. I could see out over the red-tiled roofs of the neighborhood and over toward the 20th Century Fox studio lot where the "Dolly" set still stood as a tourist attraction.

"Did you know there was a cop sitting out there, next to your door?" she asked as she took my hand and her fingers slid to my wrist. "Hold on—I'm counting." She kept her eyes on her watch.

"You're a good looking lady."

She shushed me. Then when my seconds were up, she said, "Yeah, and all nurses screw on sight."

"All humans screw. Some humans are nurses. Some nurses are female. You are a female . . . thus, you screw. Strictly Aristotle," I shrugged.

"You're right. All humans. And you're not bad . . . for an older man."

"That was low. Listen. Help me get out of here. Around that officer."

She hesitated.

"C'mon."

She nodded and reached for my clothes and spread them on the bed. "You'll have trouble raising your head after bending, so be careful of that. If you get dizzy, sit down and shove your head between your knees. You'll be OK. Your pulse is slow and regular—dammit." She pulled off my gown and I stood bald-assed naked while she retrieved my shorts and tossed them up to me. "By the way, you're not some criminal type, are you? You look harmless enough except between the navel and knees—but looks aren't everything," she mused.

"No. Just a retired private cop trying to stay retired."

While I pulled my trousers up, she said, "I don't know. I'm getting cold feet."

"C'mon. C'mon . . . you're saving a quiet man's neck. I'm a dream boat. You'll see. Write down your number. We'll check out Aristotelian syllogisms together."

"Oh, cut it out . . . I've even heard that line before." She left with a breezy smile and returned in about five minutes with a wheelchair. I put the gown around me again and she tossed a blanket over my shoulders and over my knees.

"By the way, love. What's your name?" I asked.

"Barbara. Barbara Winsher. From the famous East Side Winshers."

"I'll send a card."

We wheeled out. Barbara was efficient. It was an efficient manner rather than anything she did. A short, hefty man without a neck rose and followed us.

"Where to, nurse?" His voice was a Marlborough rattle.

Barbara explained that we were on our way to take further tests. She told the old horse which elevator and where to meet us. Patients did not take elevators with visitors, she reminded him. He bought it.

"You should command a division," I said. "It comes to you naturally."

She took me around to the parking lot. I knew I would have to wait for Elizabeth. I got up from the chair and felt faint for a moment. Removing my disguise I got into my car.

Before closing the door, I pulled Barbara to me and kissed her. "I don't know when," I said, "but sometime."

"Watch yourself," she said, "especially between the navel and the knees."

Then she left, wheelchair in front and good-looking flanks covered by my stare.

I hunched down and waited for Elizabeth, wondering why I was never really anxious to see her.

20

◆

"You up to driving?" I asked.

"I'm fine."

"Head for Tony's . . . please."

"Aren't you going to call him first?"

"No, let him be surprised."

The afternoon sun was low in the west. We took Montana Avenue east, gliding past a boutique-crazed mile of Santa Monica that sported pasta shops, croissant shops, quiche havens and women's workout-apparel shops; blue Bentleys and white Maseratis lingered at the curbsides and at boulevard stops; washed sidewalks, no trash or gum; the street signs shined. All of which was meant to impress, but like the Bentley, was merely polished, good for a glance or two and not much more. What I wanted to see was a '34 Ford V8 coupe with a rumble seat and running boards. The tinted glass silhouetted the surroundings and made everything appear burnt yellow and orange. Elizabeth drove expertly and in silence.

Finally I said, "Don't you ever work?"

"Oh, I called them from the hospital this morning and took the rest of the week off. The kids will get along without me. They'll get into my desk and steal the spelling test. That much is for sure."

"I appreciate everything, Elizabeth. I know I'm not the

best thing for your life. I have a feeling you're heading somewhere less happy than even now."

She smiled almost to herself. "We'll see."

"This is the corner," I motioned. "Turn right . . . 782 north."

I told her to pull up to the curb and sit a minute. A yellow VW squatted in the driveway. Nothing moved about the house. There was a light from a small attic window. The street was empty. Spring lawns were still green. Every other house had a magnolia tree in the parking strip, and their leaves were stretched out and their blossoms were just beyond the budding stage. I smelled honeysuckle.

I got out of the car and motioned her to stay. The doorbell was one of those old-fashioned coil-buzzer jobs that high school boys always made in their electric workshop classes.

I was being stared at. I couldn't see the eyes, but the lack of movement and the silence were good signs of it. I buzzed again and, after another full minute, William opened the curtained door. He was ashen.

"What's the matter, Bill? Something going on in there?"

"No. No. I was just feeling . . . sort of upset, you know. I'm still having nightmares." His biceps were large and I noticed again the unleashed strength in his shoulders and back. His eyes were wide but clear.

I stepped inside like a good book salesman.

"Have you seen your doctor, Bill? I think I told you to get yourself checked out."

"I don't remember that. Maybe you did. Don't like doctors." He moved closer to me. "What are you doing here?"

"Relax. I wanted to talk to your father."

"You know everything about us, for a long time now. That's so, isn't it?" And without waiting for a reply, he continued. "The police don't know the whole story. The——." He stopped. Elizabeth was standing at the door.

"Thought I'd make it a party," she said.

William turned and walked into the dining room, turned back and said, "I'm ready to go. I have to catch a class at school." He kept staring at me as if counting the seconds until we parted.

"This is Elizabeth Hume, William. She's been taking care of me, sort of."

"We've met," he said.

Elizabeth inspected my face and then turned to the boy. "I don't remember, William." She stuck her chin out at him and grunted. "Where did we meet?"

"Not exactly meet. I saw you—it's not important," he shrugged. "I've got to go. Dad's not here. You've got to leave," he said with a sudden politeness in his tone. "I'm going, so——"

"Where's your dad?"

"Out of town . . . couple of days."

I started another question, but he whirled and went into the kitchen and grabbed a ring of keys from the sink.

"He's just out of town. Be back Saturday. Didn't tell me more."

"William. I think we ought to go to the police so you can tell them your whole story in detail. You remember Lieutenant Mackin?"

"I've done all of that. *You* know everything; *I* don't. Why should I go again. Can we go now? Please?"

"I want to look around here for a while, William. Something may turn up that would help. It's just an old man's hunch."

A distant air came over him. I had seen the look before at odd times, as if he drifted to a South Sea island. He walked toward the door and waited next to Elizabeth.

"William," she said, "are you all right?"

She reached for his arm, but he jumped, and she drew back with a sudden breath. "I have to go. I'm not supposed to leave anyone here alone," he said.

"OK, we're going too, Billy," I said.

"Don't call me Billy. It's William."

"OK. William. OK." I wasn't going to fool with him. He was not the bewildered boy who had come near death at the hands of Michael Jarn and Walter Sarafin. He was angry, accumulating it inside.

As we were walking out, I asked, "That telescopic sight you have hanging on the wall in your room—do you use it?"

He looked up. "It's for my camera. I'm a camera nut, you know."

"Oh, yes. That's so. Scholarship at SC. I'll probably read about you one day when you're famous."

He locked the door and we stood on the porch a moment. "Some day," he said. He took the steps two at a time, no longer listening or caring for my reply, leaving all inquiries in limbo. His VW sprung to life with a throaty roar and he was gone.

I sat down on the porch, very tired.

Elizabeth said, "Kind of a nervous young man, no?"

I had all sorts of thoughts open and close in my brain. When I tried to create order out of the process, the pattern fizzled away. It was all on the lip of my frontal lobes, but there wasn't enough information to reach the conscious level.

"You see that light up there?" I stuck my thumb upward. "Explain it. This kind of house doesn't have a regular attic. Why is a light on?"

———————◆———————

As we drove away, Elizabeth told me about how she had met Sarafin. It seemed important to her to tell me.

She worked for an internist named Lee Kotsin who had his office in Inglewood. He had an addiction to gambling and was chummy with every trainer and jockey he could bother, as if to try to ensure getting winners. When she went to the races with Kotsin, she stared at Sarafin, Jarn approached her, and she was suddenly in his strange world. She married Jarn and within months left him and the doctor. But it was Sarafin that stuck to her.

Sarafin didn't let go. He traced her. His last love note was about a year ago. It said, "I won't forget. It will happen again. Walter."

"He'll never let me go until he owns me again," she said, somberly.

21

◆

Rainer Rilke said you have to live all your questions.

Now, again, it was time to live my questions.

A dry winter breeze carrying edges of warmth touched my face. I slipped my Chevron card into the latch, pushing away the dead nude branches of a potted ficus. The latch slipped and the door glided open as if inviting us in. Pieces of the interior were illuminated in new-moon light, blue and colder than the night.

I flipped the switch and a yellow beam spread from a narrow iron lamp.

Dried paint and lifeless stiff brushes, and eyeless canvases and flaming color leaped at me. I heard Elizabeth gasp. Ther were no recognizable forms amid the colors. Color was its own form.

Intense colors in the hot spectrum of reds and yellows dripped with tears of faded whites and distant greens. I said "schizophrenic" aloud. Some of the larger paintings had red stickers with FIRST FIDELITY written on them. An old-fashioned mantel over a fake fireplace with a gas heater in front had one picture resting on it. It was a little girl with short straight bangs sitting on the lap of a very young Henry Selmon dressed in riding silks. I looked around to see if there were more photographs. There were none. But there were small, nude white china dolls around the room on every shelf and table.

The furniture was vintage 1930: dark, brocaded, essentially uncomfortable. A thick fake fur rested on the floor in front of the gas heater. Doilies covered the armrests. The kitchen tile needed caulking but was probably seldom used for preparing food. Cans with brushes littered the countertops. A vague scent of turpentine drifted about.

I went into the bedroom, searching for the heart of Mary Jarn. Bedrooms are where hearts are customarily found—and lost. I was like an animal searching for prey.

More lace doilies. Nude china dolls in all positions. Satin sheets. Grey. An invitation. Paintings around the walls. Great swatches of color that reeked of special fires.

"Where is she?" I said almost to myself. "There's more . . . somewhere there's more."

"It better be something wonderful," Elizabeth muttered, " 'cause you are acting just like an obsessive nut."

I rifled through the drawers. Blouses and underwear and nylons and then, in the drawer in the side table by the left of the bed, I found "more."

Postcards already addressed to obvious business addresses saying, "Dear John, Dear Charles, Dear Bob—I want to do it again." And they were signed "M." And in the same drawer a handful of prostitute's panties came tumbling out, holes in the wrong places, and I wanted to laugh. Or cry. And Elizabeth said, "She was just a goddamn tramp!"

And I sank to the bed and shook my head, and didn't want to laugh and couldn't quite keep the tears in my eyes, and said over and over, "No she wasn't. She wasn't——"

"A goddamn tramp!"

"Shut up!"

She sat next to me and tried to cup my head between her palms and console me, but I was so much taller, and we fell against the table and it tumbled. A white envelope and a picture fluttered to my feet. Elizabeth reached to pick them up.

"No," I said. "Better leave it. I've had enough."

She put it on her lap. "You *have* too, Harv. You have to know . . . that's what it's all about."

There was a cross drawn in the upper corner of the envelope. William Antonnini's serious face stared out of the black-and-white snapshot that had "I love you" written on it. I slipped the blue paper out and read:

Walter,
    Never again. I'll kill you.

                                        Mary

On the way out there was an ink drawing of Mickey Mouse on the floor.

22

◆

I made Elizabeth leave. That was what I had always done.
I locked myself in my study and began to write in my
journal:

   I'm not sure what's going on but I keep chasing
   this ghost. She's on my back. . . .

Then the pen died in my hand.
I got a call from Horse Blanket Billy. He said that
Sylvia and Sarafin were together at the Del Coronado in
San Diego, that Sarafin had several visitors in the lobby
yesterday afternoon, one of whom was also registered at
the hotel. That person was Dusty Moore, a licensed pilot
with a multiengine license who was also instrument-rated.
I asked him if he could think of a way to keep Moore in
San Diego, but he told me it was too late, the leather-
jacketed Moore had checked out. I told him to come
home.
I went to the bathroom and took off my clothes, uri-
nated and then began to scrub my hands and then my
arms with a warm washcloth. I knew it was compulsive.
My head pounded. When I closed my eyes I had to hold
on. I felt better after the cleansing. I kept the lights off
and drew all the curtains and drapes. The doors were
locked. I was in my cocoon.

Waiting was deathly. I had to be the one to make it happen.

By the time I stuffed a tin of tuna down my throat, dressed, and got to my car, it was black and misty outside. One of Mackin's men waited in an unmarked Chevy down the street. I wouldn't bother to try to lose him.

I turned into Anthony Antonnini's driveway. The house felt empty and emanated death. That same dim yellow light from the attic window shot its lonely rays into the night. William's Bug wasn't in sight. My trailing and persistent policeman unrolled to a stop about 50 yards down in the shadows of a magnolia tree. He wasn't about to stop me. I was doing his dirty work. No warrant and no advising a suspect of constitutional rights.

I poked a finger through a rusty screen in the back, shoved the window up and pulled myself into the house. Locating the source of light, an attic aperture in the closet ceiling in William's room, I approached with painful awareness. I didn't like the idea of inserting myself into a hole in the ceiling while I was in danger of another dizzy spell, but there was no choice. I was mesmerized by the light.

Placing a chair under the trapdoor, I half-expected a monstrous intruder to lumber in and attack. I felt terribly exposed. Shoving aside the board that doubled as a door for the passage, I pulled myself up into the narrow space. My pupils contracted in the light. There was three feet of space in a gentle A-frame shape. Dust rustled into the air from my movements. Cardboard cartons spilled from one another around the edges of the room.

Lying atop a row of the cartons was Sam Rosenstock. He reclined peacefully, but he wasn't sleeping. I crawled to him. He was dressed in street clothes, blue slacks, white polo shirt and a soft wool sweater. It was as if he had gone out for a while to walk the dog. There was a not-so-neat hole in his forehead. The blood around his head was already dried. A trail of blood followed him to his resting place from where I had entered the attic. Blood had trickled down his nose, a line of life dried up, one that could be washed away. Blood encrusted his sweater.

Poor Sam. Mary, Cyril Weber and now Sam, and I was sure they were mere bystanders. I couldn't think of him as *Sammy* any more. His curiosity and his job combined to put him into a situation of risk that he did not comprehend. Undoubtedly, my earlier call had gotten him deeper into an inquiry that he had already begun.

On the floor in a corner was a long brown felt bag. I untied the straps and unfurled a carefully manufactured Winfrey .22 caliber rifle with a hookup for a sight.

As I eased myself down the attic I felt my head buzz and a nausea sweep over me. And I had to lower myself to the floor before I fell. I pushed my head down and held it there. Why was the light left on? Was I supposed to be a moth? I had been drawn to that light since my visit with William. If I had been set up, it would all be over in a few minutes.

Listening and breathing carefully I knit myself together. Sam must have tied Tony Antonnini into the dope-sale transaction. Or did he tie him into the death of Mary Jarn? It was foreseeable except for one thing: there was no apparent reason for Sam not to cooperate with the LAPD, and no reason for him to be sleuthing around on his own unless there was some personal involvement. Unless part of $100 million was his temptation and his downfall. Or unless he was betrayed.

I followed blood smudges from William's room to the back porch. There were no hand or finger marks on any of the doors or handles. I went back and began to search William's room. The telescopic sight was not on the wall. Other than that empty wall space, there was nothing to guide my thoughts.

I thumbed through a stack of carelessly gathered correspondence. *Newsweek* wanted a subscription. Arco was having a contest. There was a gun catalog from a shop in Pasadena, a bill from a psychiatrist, and an announcement from the Forester Park Softball League. The psychiatrist's bill was dated yesterday: $400 for four sessions last November and December. I noticed that the invoice was from a psychiatrist, not a psychologist. In the dark I dialed the doctor's number.

My gut told me that Mackin would be knocking at the door to the house in a matter of minutes. I memorized the number and name, tore the bill into four pieces, put a match to it, and dumped it into a metal waste basket.

"Dr. Hanish?"

His voice was already perturbed. "Yes. Who is this, please? It's very late."

"You don't know me, but I had to talk to you immediately. The name is Ace. Harvey Ace."

"I don't want to know you, Mr. Ace, unless this is a social call. It's very late."

"I don't know if you would consider a murder strictly social or not; however, that's what I want to talk about."

There was a short, empty space of time.

"I don't want to know about it, Mr. Ace. Try to understand, there's only so much I want to know about anything. Goodnight."

I spoke hurriedly, wanting to capture his thoughts before I was cut off. "I think William Antonnini is on a killing rampage and . . . I think that you or I are probably on his list."

"That's nonsense. Who are you, anyway? Explain yourself now or I'm calling in the police. Tell me——"

"The police are on their way. Bill Antonnini is a patient of yours and is more than a little neurotic, right?"

Another empty space of time.

I went on. "I need to know whether he is under some

compulsion or obsession, or whether he is acting in some calculated way."

"Tell me who you are?"

"A friend of his father's. As far as I can tell his father is in danger, too."

I lied. If William was someone's killing device, or if he was his own crazed, misguided Mary Jarn avenger, he would never harbor the thought of harming his father. Nevertheless, it seemed to stop the doctor.

"Has an attempt been made on Mr. Antonnini's life?"

"Just answer me, please, Dr. Hanish. There isn't a lot of time."

"I can't tell you anything. You know that——."

"That's crap," I said. "You can tell me everything just by the tone of your voice, by an inflection, by a question. Is the Antonnini boy sick enough to kill people? A weird sicko?"

"Weird sickos are usually in the hospital, by order of their doctor, aren't they?"

"Are they?"

"Well, perhaps not always."

"That's what I thought."

"I don't want to talk to you or listen to you anymore. So far as I'm concerned, you never called. I don't know you and don't call back—for any reason."

"Sooner or later the police will be calling."

The line growled dead.

I thought, I don't want to be here. I was lured to the light. But now I don't want to go out. There was only an unmarked car down the street with a cop inside wondering what the hell I was doing in this place and wishing he was in front of "Police Story" reruns.

I stuck my index finger in 6 on the dial and slowly twirled Lew Mackin's home number.

The line kept ringing, over and over. Then I called his office number and was told he was out on assignment.

Glancing into the street from the edge of the living room door I saw a desolate, lazy strip of West Hollywood: old framed houses, peaked windows with curtained dreams drifting out of quiet rooms.

I sat and waited for something to happen. When you don't know what to do, you make waiting the same as doing. In a few minutes a black and white eased up to the curb.

Mackin's jowls were unshaven. He was with another officer who was built like an icebox. I explained the last two hours.

"Why didn't you call?"

"I tried. You aren't home and aren't at the office."

"OK, let's go."

"No, Mack. I don't want to."

"The meat wagon is coming, Harv," he said quietly. "Nothing more can happen to Sam."

"What about me?"

He looked at me as if I were an interesting beetle that had wandered into his path.

23

It took forever to complete Mack's report. I wanted to cooperate with him. I wanted to work out a deal giving me space within which to operate. I did not want the LAPD to assume control, because bureaucracies are inherently deficient in fine-tuning. On the other hand, they could cover all the bases. There would be one catch: I had indulged in it both in the army and since—*I* would be the bait. It wasn't my style. I didn't mind using someone else as bait, but I couldn't imagine being in that spot. You controlled nothing, not a second of your own breath. So I held back.

Lew knew what I was thinking. He taught me the game. But he didn't push. He grunted and answered the phone, and grunted and gave instructions. He started to try to trace Tony Antonnini—first all airlines, then a call to San Diego police and to Customs describing Tony and the car he was driving, and then put out an APB. He did the same for William. He tried to reach Hank Selmon with no success, and I was angry inside because Hank told me that he would stay put.

Finally he grunted again, loosened his belt, and nodded at me. "I wish you would let me handle it, Harv."

"You know better, Mack."

"I do, but I also know what's best. I also know that

I'm not gonna let you go on and on like this. I want you away. Locked up, if need be."

"Do you honestly want me to play your game?" I asked. "Because if so——"

"Go on home, Harvey," Mackin interrupted, and held his arms up and rolled his head. "Believe it or not, we're not nearly as bad as we used to be."

"I need that information on my cast of characters like you promised."

He shoved his hand into the bowels of his top desk drawer and handed me one double-spaced typewritten sheet. It read: "Walter Sarafin born 1920, August 3, Vaizo, Turkey. Father: Captain Armandi Sarafin, Turkish Army, WWI. Mother: Cecilia Schtellenheim, German, daughter of German colonel assisted Allies in administering remnants of Ottoman Empire. Subject raised in interior. Substantial wealth, farming. Suspected grower and processor of opiates. U.S. citizen, 1958. Married and divorced in U.S. 1967—Florence Childs, New York. One child of prior marriage, 29 years. Male, resides in Antwerp, Belgium. Varied local business interests. Travels. No arrest record. FBI suspects international narcotics dealing. No deportation proceeding contemplated. Checking further."

I folded the sheet into fours. "If I need more, I'll take a chance and call."

"Take all the chances you want. It's not my problem. I've got only 101 days left. It's enough on my head just thinking about that." He smiled a tired, knowing smile. His eyes closed. "I want you out of this situation, Harv."

At home I entered information on the appropriate cards, reminded myself to get the window fixed, and then read my own card, in my own handwriting, about Sam Rosenstock: "Born 1913, Washington's birthday in Los Angeles, Queen of Angels Hospital. Resided in Watts area. (It was then middle-class white neighborhood along

Red Car line.) Golden Gloves Middleweight champ 1932. Pro boxer, local—Long Beach, San Diego. Boxed 10 years. Worked wire service for bookmakers 1936. Arrested bookmaking 1937. Dismissed. No license problem. Two fights Chicago and five fights St. Louis. National ranking. Reputation big hitter, no finesse. Married Helene Finkel 1936. Two daughters, three grandchildren. Helene cooks lasagne in special way. Security officer Santa Anita, Del Mar. Chief of Security, Del Mar, 1973. Attended Los Angeles City College night school to qualify. Son-in-law movie producer. Big bookmaking record overlooked—guess: son-in-law pulled right ropes."

I added: "Died July 7, 1987. Surviving wife, two daughters and three grandchildren."

Then I checked my revolver, holstered it, shut off all the lights, and stared out into the black that was sky and ocean fused into one screen of darkness. Nothing. But my hunter was near. I knew it.

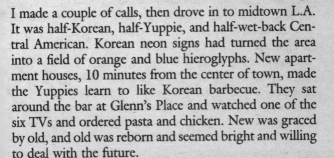

I made a couple of calls, then drove in to midtown L.A. It was half-Korean, half-Yuppie, and half-wet-back Central American. Korean neon signs had turned the area into a field of orange and blue hieroglyphs. New apartment houses, 10 minutes from the center of town, made the Yuppies learn to like Korean barbecue. They sat around the bar at Glenn's Place and watched one of the six TVs and ordered pasta and chicken. New was graced by old, and old was reborn and seemed bright and willing to deal with the future.

I slipped the lock and I let myself into Mackin's apartment just off 4th Street at New Hampshire. Good building. Mackin's living room was a place to sit and watch TV. There were two of them. A tweed couch, the shade of shredded wheat, tried to hide under a half-dozen brown and ocher pillows, painfully empty bookshelves stared from the opposite wall, a desk with a used coffee cup in the middle sat in one corner near the sliding door to a small patio and to the dining area and kitchen beyond. A door to a hallway and bathroom led to the bedroom.

Automatically I began to stack his dishes and wipe off the sink and tabletops. I wondered who owned the Porsche that sped away when I killed Michael Jarn. And I wondered if whoever was after me was also after Walter Sarafin. It seemed to me that I had been shoved into the middle of a perfectly operating conspiracy. I would never forget Mary Jarn's body at my feet—white, staring, lost.

I searched everywhere seeking the missing bolt that made the machine work.

Later, at home, asleep on the couch, the phone rang me awake and Mackin said, "Please don't snoop, Mr. Ace. You know it's unconstitutional."

"Sorry, Lew. I don't even know what I was looking for."

"Just an old war-horse—"

"Not just that. I have this feeling, Lew—nothing to go on, no justification—that in some way you're involved in this mess."

Silence. Fifteen seconds on my second hand. Then: "Harvey, don't speculate. Just get lost. Wait. One last bit of info for you. Then maybe you'll be done with your crazy ideas. Tony was the owner of the apartment house in Newport. His kid is a dead-eye from ROTC. Make any sense? Anyway, keep ducking."

24

◆

I telephoned Henry Selmon's house. No answer. I telephoned Tony Antonnini's house. No answer. I poached a couple of eggs and slid them onto a half of an English muffin and watched the yellow ooze languidly around the edges. I tried to keep my diet to four eggs a week, convinced that diet was the key to fame and fortune. I just never could find the precise diet that would do the trick.

I showered, threw a clean towel on the floor of the bathroom and then took a washcloth and scrubbed my hands again until they glowed red.

Before leaving, I put all the dishes into the washer and wiped the ivory tile counter.

On the way to Del Mar I tried to recall all the details of the past few weeks, and I reminded myself that it was important to be at Sam Rosenstock's funeral.

Later, I inserted into my journal:

For some reason, Antonnini wants me dead and alive at the same time. I'm being used by him or whoever directs him. Yet I remember when Tony was real to me, when his sadness was played out on a piano keyboard, when everything was gentle, and when you could only suspect that he might be slowly going mad—a model for his own son. But he isn't the key to this. I've got to review my notebooks again.

South of Laguna you could see fifty miles out into the shining sea, shimmering quietly past fields of bluebonnets that lead to edge of the bluffs above a pacified morning ocean.

When I got to the track I asked Sasha Lopez to park my car so that I could leave in a hurry. "You see Hank Selmon's car, Sash?" I asked, as I handed him a larger than usual bill.

He stroked his mustache, thought a minute, tightened his cap on his forehead, and said, "Yeah. . . ." He stared at me. "He's a little but nuts, ya know. One second he's giggling, and the next he's screamin' about nothin'. Just between us: too much shit in his system. Not enough frijoles, OK? Your car will be along the pathway aiming out. Right there." He tilted his chin toward the spot.

"OK, Sash. If Selmon leaves early, try to get someone to tell me, will you?"

Two fingers waved a salute as he pulled away.

I asked sour-faced Leon, the maître d' in the Turf Club, if he had seen Walter or Tony. He shook his head and asked if I wanted a table while it was still early. I told him no, then looked for Fred and found him in a circle of ticket clerks, their red vests making them look like sloppy waiters.

"Where you working today, Fred?"

His round face spread into warmth. No spilled guilt on his soul, I thought.

"Hiya, Harv. I'm at the $10 windows today. Harry and John got the big ones. Got somethin' today, Harv?"

"Could be. But I'm looking for Hank Selmon. He been around?"

"Haven't seen him. Not for a while, either. C'mon, Harv. Tell us, we'll keep it in the family."

Shaking my head, I said, "I'll be in the bar. Do me a special favor and let me know when Hank shows up. By the way, if you see Billy send him over."

He curled his thumb and index finger into an OK.

The bar was green—carpeting, paint, pots, plants, couches, chairs. Television sets encircled it, with first-race odds in white on a blue background.

Charlie Zorn handed me a bottled Tab and nodded. He waited, then asked me if I knew about Sam Rosenstock. I had heard, I told him. He put a glass with ice in front of me and said, "I never knew a Jewish cop before, did you?

"In Europe. They went around flushing out Nazis . . . sometimes from under my nose. I used to need those damn Nazis to get their country running again. But they didn't spare me many."

He grunted. "I liked Sammy."

"That's nice." My voice was thick with sarcasm.

"I'd like to shove your disposition up your ass, Ace. Don't drink my coke if you think I'm some kind of racist." He was leaning toward me.

I told him I was sorry, and his anger left as quickly as it had come.

I thought I saw something familiar catch the corner of my eye. I twisted the stool around. Nothing.

I wasn't satisfied.

I walked against the grain toward the stairs that erupted into the Turf Club. Down the stairs and into the main paddock and garden area. I made my eyes circle the farthest ends of the courtyard as the crowd grew heavier, busier as it passed me. My view went up the ivy-covered cracked stuccoed walls, to the wrought-iron railing beneath three Spanish arches that framed the Turf Club's open-air dining room.

Once again there was a quick movement. Dishes clattered and fell. I ran back to the stairway clawing through the traffic, up the stairs again, through the bar and out to the grandstand. The world was bright and summer green.

I stood, not breathing for a moment, with a sense of having been played with. I tried using my eyes as binoculars, checking each area of the stands above me. Then I went back to the bar as the track announcer began to read the changes for each race.

In the first three races, there was one overweight and no scratches. In the fourth, Pincay's horse had to carry 117 pounds instead of the 114 pounds assigned. Pincay couldn't ride at less than 117 pounds. In the fifth, Ring Spring was scratched.

The crowd built up. Daily Double lines grew. I divorced the bar and went into the general-admission grandstand area. I had to keep moving. Sarafin's box was still empty. If I found Tony Antonnini or Hank Selmon I might be able to call the next turn of the cards. I was certain there were dangerous cards yet to be played.

Concrete stairs led to a corridor in the lower portion of the stands. The personnel and racing secretary's offices lined each side. At the distant end, stairs led upward toward the far turn of the track at the field level where the horses flung themselves into the last charge home.

I was halfway up when I heard shuffling behind me. This time I turned in time. Tony Antonnini came at me with a left-hook lead. No time for jabs.

"You gotta stay outta the way, Harv," he grunted.

The blow caught me in the right rib cage and snuffed the air out. I couldn't counter with a right and crouched as low as I could, and he come down on my neck, stunning me and the Marquis de Queensberry at the same time. I pushed into him, lowering my left shoulder, and came up with a right. I was a step above him so I missed the soft part of his belly and hit his chest. I wanted to grab him and hold on and talk to him, but there was no stopping this. He couldn't chance my interference. There was no leverage above him and I stepped down into him. As I did, he came down on my instep with a heavy jerk and up into my belly in one fluid movement.

My god, I thought, I'm getting beaten up. I can't get untracked. I started to wobble down the rest of the stairs. I grabbed him in a bear hug. I only managed to muffle his pumping areas. As my body began to slip backward down the stairs, I caught his collar and pulled hard. We tumbled.

My head hit the bottom with a cracking flash. Midnight hit my eyes for a second. I held on to the collar. I heard Antonnini grunt and swear. I tried to use my weight to roll over.

"Stay away, Ace!" I heard. "Stay away. For god's sake, stay out of it." Then I heard him say, "Please . . ."

I kept thinking, that's gratitude for you, but couldn't say it.

I felt a bang on my ear. I was aware of everything but couldn't get my eyes to function or my arms to swivel or get myself set. My head banged against the cement again. I felt nausea and dizziness returning. I rolled over, my nose now facing China. I heard shouting. Suddenly I was free. Tony was retreating as fast as he had attacked. If he was trying to hurt me, he succeeded. If he was trying to damage me, he failed.

A thunder of vertigo shuddered over me. A frontal assault in the business of stealth was a mistake, I thought. I would have used an iron pipe on his forearm . . . reparable, but a blow that put one out of action for three to four days. Slowly, the grey lifted from the rear of my eyes. I began to tune in. I recalled the doctor's caution and sat on the cement floor and put my head between my knees.

It was a good ten minutes before I began to feel better. The attack was typical of a fighter. Everything could be settled with the fist. I often wondered what it would be like if I had settled my affairs with my father by fists. I remembered my father's fists. They were puny. Even then, when I was very young, I knew they were not very theatening. Poor man. He used to come in the door precisely at 6:35 each evening, except Fridays when he came home at 9:35, banging the springless screen door shut, standing at parade rest waiting for my mother and myself to present ourselves. Then he would smack his right fist into his left palm and say, "It's power that counts. A fist in time saves nine!" I never knew what the hell he meant, but my mother would open his fist with her fingers, one by one, put his open hand on her bosom and say, "Sons must disappear when fathers appear, Harvey." And I would exit and try to figure out what it all meant.

I struggled upstream back to the Turf Club.

There were long lines and anxious faces, wrinkled brows over programs and tip sheets and the *Racing Form,* the smell of hot dogs just like on a hot summer baseball night, and the call of the announcer: "The horses will reach the starting gate in fi-eve minutes."

I saw Bob Galliant, horse picker and bookwriter. He pointed at Sylvia's Secret in the sixth race in his program. It made me angry. I didn't want the horse to win. His black forested eyebrows bounced up and down, and he pointed at Walter Sarafin when I asked.

Before going to his box, I edged carefully through the humanity to the track hospital. Doc Pinner jumped when I tapped his shoulder.

"Do you have to sneak up on a person?" he demanded, Band-Aid in hand. He sat up onto one of his examining tables and took off his left black smooth shoe. "Dammit, Harvey. I knew you would be here. But that's no way to treat a friend."

"I didn't mean it, Doc. I didn't realize I was going to surprise you. Why were you expecting me?"

He contemplated my face and smiled. "There was a fight, right?"

"Yes."

"So it had to be you. Who else would get into a brawl in fancy duds?" His free hand slapped my lapel as the other peeled off his sock. "Look at you, for chrissakes. Bleeding from the head, but trousers perfectly creased and still clean. I'm suspicious of well-groomed people. You didn't even bleed into your collar."

"What are you doing, Doc?"

He pointed with a flourish. "There. See? The damn toe is rubbed raw. It's killing me. What if an emergency came in and I had to use my feet? Then what?"

I shrugged helplessly. He continued. "Somehow, that girl's death and Sam's murder and you are all rolled up into one. Right? Well, I'm right, whatever you answer. The police have a half-dozen men around. Everyone seems to be waiting. It's fitting for a place like this." He finished with his toe and then examined my head and made my eyes follow his finger. "Seems like you keep stepping into piles of shit, Harv. And you come up clean. But the odds are getting shorter, aren't they?"

I told him I would remember and that I would try not to take one step too many in the future. He said, "Don't try. It won't work."

25

◆

I stood staring at Mr. and Mrs. Walter Sarafin as they sat quietly in their box. They were alone. Darkness lurked between them, sitting there, framed by the tranquil green patch of life in the center of the racing oval.

Two men stood at the railing above the Sarafins' box. One had skin like an aerial view of a volcanic island; the other was slim and young; both were in dark suits.

I waited until Sylvia slipped quietly away into the betting crowd. Then I approached and fitted myself into the chair next to Sarafin. "You called, I believe."

His head barely turned, and he threw me a courtesy upward curl of his lips. "That's right." His voice had its vague accent, not definable unless you knew its travels. "I didn't think you would show up, Mr. Ace," he said.

"Did you have special reasons?"

"No. Well, perhaps. Perhaps the same reasons you had when you visited me a couple nights ago."

"Three nights ago."

"Was it only three? Seems like much more," he mused, "much more."

"Did your wife leave by request, or does she have a winner?"

"I asked her to leave. Saw you pass here from the grandstand. You waited," he turned his watch toward his suspended grey eyes, "almost eight minutes before approaching."

"No. You waited almost ten minutes before sending her away or asking her to leave. And it was an interesting ten minutes."

He smiled again. "How so?"

"Neither of you spoke. Not a word."

He laughed a quick, curt laugh. He seemed very sure of himself. "That's why I called you," he said. "You are keen enough to get things done and curious enough to accept a useless challenge."

"It would suit me if you didn't bother with the analysis. I've had enough of that. I analyze you as scared stiff. On the edge of doing something foolish. Else I wouldn't be here. And you wouldn't be so cool . . . on the outside."

I looked around. Heads bobbed. Colors flashed. Life hung on the fingers of $2 pari-mutuel clerks. The clatter of the machines collided with waves of human noise.

"It's not a good idea to insult me, Ace. I snap my fingers and insults disappear."

"I suggest you get on with it then, Sarafin. There's nothing you can say that will change anything. So let's quit sparring and get on with it."

"You were shot at," he said. "I can see the mark above your ear." He looked at me with a direct, clear stare. "And you've been threatened, and rumor has it, beaten. I don't understand why you're still around. But I suppose you like your style of living."

"You seem to like it—you're so interested in it."

He turned, almost wearily substituting boredom for insult. "I'm not even slightly interested, Ace. I have my own problems. I've got horses that run poorly, friends who pout ——"

"And lovers?"

Not missing a beat he continued, "——partners who aren't, trainers who disappear, riders who drop their stick, a tired stock market, businesses that convulse when the Federal Reserve sneezes, and someone who is trying to kill me for reasons I haven't been able to fathom."

I had made a believer out of him. One hundred mil' was too much to keep in absolute control.

"And that's why you called me?"

His lips thinned, increasing the cruelty of his face. He belonged to a special world. It owned him. He couldn't possess a style of life. It possessed him.

I told him what I believed his schemes were. I laid it out from Mary Jarn to Ring Spring to money, dope and Sam Rosenstock. Half of it was pure speculation. Then I told him that I was certain that he was not likely to live more than a few days.

The essential flaw in his character came through. Deep down where it counts, he had no morality. There were no standards charting his course except what suited his purposes at the moment. The ultimate psychopath. Like a man dying too slowly, he didn't believe in anything but living.

"Those horses out there have more meaning to me than your threats. You have no validity with me."

I rose. "Thanks for the good words. I've got better things to do."

"Hold on. Hold on. Now just hold on." He put his hand on my sleeve and I pulled it back. "Now, now. I want to talk to you. We've been spending our time disliking each other." He tried to chuckle. "Too much energy, really. I have need of you and you of me. And money *does* talk."

"Not to me. I play the horses. For fun, not profit."

"Please, please. Sit down. Please—before Sylvia comes back."

Doc Pinner was right. I can never resist. I sat down.

"Somebody is trying to kill me and to kill you. Each of us is a target, and I know it and you know it, and I

have the same interest as you: keeping alive—and well."
His eyes darted around. He moved his hand and his
guards moved two steps away. "One of my friends or
associates has decided I'm in the way. How that can be
is beyond me, because, really, I hold the—you say—purse
strings. But, it seems, there's no loyalty in this world.
None at all. Truthfully, I'm not concerned about the
reasons anyone wants *you* dead. Unless it helps you find
and kill him before he does it to me—or to you, of
course."

"Or *she* does it—"

His nose turned slowly into the grey racing form, not
acknowledging my remark. A bell sang into the air. The
crowd lifted itself up, reaching out for its thrills. The
sweet sound of straining thoroughbreds rose from below.
I automatically rose to watch the race.

"C'mon, get up," I said. "I want both of us exposed
right now. Not just me. Get up." He tossed his head at
the two men behind us. They came closer. The one with
the ancient acne kept pulling at his ear. Sarafin gazed
back, eyes all grey and shallow. "That one speaks Turkish
and Armenian. But no English. I could tell him to break
your arm right now, and you wouldn't know." The level
of his voice rose. "I also speak French quite well and can
understand Arabic." He was shouting without realizing
it in order to be heard above the noise.

"Sarafin, the Turkish Palace Guard couldn't stop an
assassin if he announced the time and place." I grabbed
his binoculars, which were strapped around a folding
chair, and watched #7 pull out in the stretch and glide
home. "Now that we understand each other . . ." I said,
as the hum of the race sank into the clatter of dishes and
the sliding of chairs on linoleum as people settled in to
prepare for the next race.

"You're right. We do understand each other. I don't
want to go on with this fencing. I'm willing to pay you

very well to find your own assassin. It's a novel proposition. Kill him and collect $10,000. Simple. Novel and simple." He tried to conjure up an easy smile, but it came across his face as an insecure twist with teeth.

"I don't need $10,000. I need the person who murdered Mary Jarn."

He put his binoculars to his eyes. "You have drawn stupid conclusions. You believe I am an international fiend killing at the drop of a hat or by a mere nod of my head. Whatever you have concluded by the story you told me, banish the thoughts. You're 70 percent wong and the other 30 percent, misguided. I'm in the racing business, the trucking business, the paper business—and others."

"I want what I want."

He continued. "Twenty thousand dollars. I think we both need to stay alive. Money in advance, of course. Could you successfully save both our necks?"

"Very successfully."

"Well," he said, "I'm too old to begin to leave hanging wires."

"Mr. Sarafin. Up in that crowd behind us is Elizabeth Hume. I believe you knew her. One time she was Elizabeth Jarn. Also in the crowd is a police detective very interested in every move I make. On one hand, the lady has a pistol big enough to drill a tunnel through your rear dimensions, and on the other hand the detective is a good friend. That means to me that our mystery person is unknown to us. Not those up there."

"You could be wrong."

I turned, smiled, and waved into the crowd. I hadn't the foggiest idea where Elizabeth actually was, but I knew she was back there somewhere. She was always at the right place. "I don't want your money. You are in a bind. That's the way I figure it."

I searched his face. I expected to find some psychic

trauma in it, an ability to penetrate beyond the retina of the eyes. It wasn't there. It wasn't in him.

"You're dead as far as I'm concerned," he said. "If you can't help me, you are in the way. So I consider you dead—you can get out of my sight now." His voice had grown hoarse. "Out of my sight."

"I see your wife coming anyway." I stepped out of the box, trying to smile.

"You are dead, Ace. Remember that."

"Not before you. You first, baby. You first."

Sylvia Sarafin touched my shoulder as she slipped past, descending tightly into her chair. "My horse is the winner in this race, Mr. Ace. My secret horse." Then she stopped, felt the tension surrounding us. "Oh, you two have been at it again, haven't you? You must enjoy it."

She shook her head, tossing her hair out like the slow-motion effect in one of those Clairol ads. A watermelon-colored silk fabric attached itself closely about her body. Her dark eyes gathered in the light. They had an unfinished intensity. I thought she was the most clearly unfinished creature I had ever encountered. It made her unpredictable. That was her catalytic process: unpredictability.

"Won't you stay and watch my filly anyway, Mr. Ace?"

"No. I won't stay, and she won't win. I can guarantee it."

"No wonder you get along so well with Walter. You have such a sweet disposition." She held up her program. "Oh, go away, Mr. Ace," she said suddenly. "Go away."

All at once I recognized that she was vulnerable and ready to blurt out a special truth. It was written luminously across her face. She was about to speak, but Sarafin's hand reached over and covered his wife's fingers, closing over them slowly. I turned away. I didn't care what went on between them. I knew what he could do.

26

The sixth race was an Allowance race for three-year-old fillies that hadn't won two races except Maiden or Claiming races. The purse was $12,000, and the distance was six furlongs, three-quarters of a mile. The record at Del Mar was 1:07 3/5. These fillies had some promise. All of them had been in the winner's circle. For a good filly, winning was intoxicating. The crowd's roar made their ears flick and their rumps bounce. Mid-year was the time that the genuinely good fillies showed their quality. They had become full grown, had beaten illness and injury during the most susceptible time of their lives, and were still ready and able to run. After a win in an Allowance of this sort, you could expect a few Handicap Feature races and an occasional stakes race and some important money.

Sylvia's Secret was one of seven fillies in the race. She had the third post position and was 8 to 5 at the opening. She had finished second in her last race and had won the prior two, one of them in December at Santa Anita as a two-year-old. She had Simrin up who was on a hot streak. My Girl was #1 at 5 to 1; Grandma #2 at 8 to 1; Turning Lady #4 at 4 to 1; Dancing Down #5 at 5 to 2; Wake Up #6 at 7 to 2; and Lullaby Keed #7 at 5 to 1.

My Girl had won her last in 1:10 flat by two lengths. She had a tendency to drift so she had blinkers on for the first time. Grandma hadn't won since Churchill Downs in April and had been beaten badly two weeks earlier in a very classy race against already proven company. In spite of her poor showing, her speed was good; she was just outdistanced. The time before last, even though she drifted toward the middle of the track, she placed a good third in 1:10 1/5. Turning Lady had special breeding: she was by Gaelic Dancer, a proven stud. She had been a super two-year-old at Aqueduct and had come west and flunked twice at Hollywood Park. But she worked at :47 flat two days earlier and 1:12 1/5 four days before that. She was better than her last two races. And breeding is a factor that must be considered.

Dancing Down came last on July 3 but had won her prior two races, just as Sylvia's Secret had. In Dancing Down's maiden race she had coasted in, galloping easily at 1:10 4/5, then had a third, and then won again in a $40,000 claiming race. She probably was of Allowance caliber at Golden Gate or Pomona but seemed over her head here. Wake Up was by TV Lark, an extremely successful stud. Her mother was by Windy Sands, who was a superior sprinter. Wake Up had won her last race in 681:09 4/5, but hadn't raced since the spring, and her workouts were unrevealing. She had won only the one race in which was a maiden, although she had raced twice before.

A prime betting rule is not to bet a winner of a maiden race next time around. The competition in such a race is just not stiff enough to be a good test . . . . Except you can never tell when there is going to be an exception. You judge a good horse by the company it keeps. At the last post position, #7, Lullaby Keed seemed to have the keenest speed of all for the first half-mile. She had won her maiden and had come in second three times in a row. If you totaled the distance of her losses it might be as much as a half-length. She had Pincay up, too, which was a special plus.

Turning Lady went to 10 to 1. Dancing Down was at 8 to 1, Wake Up was at 4 to 1, and Sylvia's Secret was at 6 to 5. If TV Lark horses stay healthy, they get better. Windy Sands's offspring may not do well at a mile, but at six furlongs they are tough. If Lullabye Keed took the front from the outside post it was probable she would fade at the middle of the turn, with or without Pincay.

Wake Up had speed in her bones, not just on the training track. I suspected that Turning Lady was flashy in the workouts and had grown early as a two-year-old but was nothing much now. The favorite looked on paper to be the proper choice. She stayed off the pace a little, moved in the stretch and in general seemed to do things right. And Selmon was a first-rate trainer. But I didn't want that filly to win. I didn't want that animal to finish the race. If I had to push my horse over the line first, I would.

I saw "Nails." His fingernails grew out three-quarters of an inch from each finger. He never touched you. And his fingers never touched anything. The nails glistened like crystal claws as he told me that he had covered the favorite pretty good but had to try Pincay's horse in case of a runaway. I never discussed my choices with anyone, but this time I had to.

"Tough race," I said.

His fat nose bobbled as he used a left index nail to scratch it. "They should ban these races," he said.

"Don't bet."

"Umm."

"How about #6?" I asked, as if inquiring about the weather.

He looked up at me. A mole under his left eye thrust out four white hairs. God, you're ugly, Nails, I thought.

"Number 6 comes third. Lay off the race, Harv. Didn't

you just get the lowdown from Sarafin? He's W. S. Stables, you know. That three horse looks too good."

"He's not going to know the time of day by tonight," I said. Then I laughed. "Whatever that means."

I caught Elizabeth out of the corner of my eye standing inside near the bar.

"Why are you asking me?" Nails asked. "You *never* ask me. *I* should do as well as you do."

"No," I told him. "Do like I *say* and not like I do . . . 'cause I'm crazy. Did you know that? See that beauty there—over there—thinking she can hide from me? I'm going to send her out of my life. You want to watch, Nails?"

He stepped away. "You're crazy, Harvey. I always knew it, too."

I turned at the same time and jumped four steps toward Elizabeth who froze before I got to her. She didn't resist as I pulled her arm and waved at Nails and smiled. The nails on his left hand reached like pincers at a blue handkerchief in his breast pocket. It hung from the end of his hand as if by magic. He dabbed at his nose and then across his forehead. He didn't let me watch him replace it, and it annoyed me. Instead, he gave me the finger, curled a grin under his shining nose and flipped his back to me.

"You're holding me too damn tight, Harvey."

"Tell me, Elizabeth. Talk to me."

"You're hurting me. Please."

I eased up.

She said, "I'm chasing after you. I love you . . . fool. But you're so damn busy with Sarafin and his crew——." She wrenched away.

The trumpeter sounded the call of the race. I wanted to see the colors and how each animal behaved. You can see the washy horses and know that they may be sweating away their best race.

"You shouldn't be in my life," she said.

"For a change you're right."

I went out to the deck. The first jockey wore light-blue silks, the second hot pink and diagonal black stripes. Sylvia Sarafin's filly had her own blood-red and grey combination with a red cap. Yellow was next. Then black and white dots. Wake Up, #6, wore pale green with a pink rose on the back and a matching saddle cloth. Lullabye Keed wore chartreuse. I tried not to remember the colors of each number. For me it was bad luck. I just let the color invade my soul. I held Elizabeth close to me and watched the Sarafins and the odds. They had settled: Sylvia's Secret #3 at 6 to 5, #5 at 7 to 2, and #6 at 9 to 2. The Gaelic Dancer filly got a little action and moved down to 8 to 1. The one horse was lathered up. Much too nervous. The six horse plodded; and I worried.

All I knew was that I wanted to beat #3. I could taste it. Elizabeth kept trying to interrupt. I kept telling her to hold it. I pulled her with me as I went to the windows and waited. Soon Sylvia approached. The two women caught each other in a black glance.

Elizabeth tugged at my elbow and turned away. "C'mon, Harvey. Please."

I was reminded suddenly about that moment before the death of Mary Jarn. The tug at my sleeve.

Sylvia said, "Would you like to join us in the winner's circle after the race, Mr. Ace?"

"No, thanks, Mrs. Sarafin. Besides," I said airily, "This one is mine—not yours."

"You wish."

"That's right. I wish."

"I don't understand, Mr. Ace. You have no stake in this race—or in me. I've done my very best to be pleasant and helpful. I'm not indebted to you. Or to your friend."

"I don't know about your debts——"

Elizabeth interrupted. "Henry Selmon was a good kid.

You made him a hype. You and that sonofabitch-
ing——."

I grabbed her and pressed her face into my shoulder.

Sylvia commanded the space between us. She was stiff
with anger. The thinness of her face made her seem like
a suddenly haggard Nefertiti. "No one made Henry Selmon what he is," she said. "He did it all himself. Just
remember that. And you're the one who needs to be
afraid. Not me." Her index finger chopped upward. "Remember that——" She whirled, skirt swirling about her
fine knees. She ordered a stream of $50 win tickets on
#3.

Fred smiled and punched away.

I stood in the next line and ordered twenty $100 tickets
on #6, just loud enough for Sylvia Sarafin to hear. Fred
looked up. He gave me a quizzical look as if my credibility
had been suddenly stripped away. Perhaps it had. When
you are young there is life in every sunset and sunrise,
all nights are warm, all mornings have special expecta-
tions, the sky is always alive with flutterings and vibrant
with blue mutations. Perhaps I was reaching the time of
life when I might finally admit who and what I was. Not
to the world, never. Just to myself. And perhaps I had
learned that life does hurt and that there are only questions.

I heard the announcer say, "Five minutes to post time,"
and took Elizabeth's hand. She had surrendered to my
preoccupation and I had tabled my curiosity about her
presence.

My horse went to 4 to 1, then 7 to 2, and then back
to 4 to 1. We stood above the finish line. I put the tickets
in my left jacket breast pocket. It was the luckiest spot
in the ensemble. I said to myself, "Wake Up, c'mon home,
baby. First is the only way."

The horses skittered into the starting gate. Number 4
had to be shoved in, and after the gates closed the starter

hesitated. My Girl tried to escape the prison. Even without the glasses I could see the grey felt hat and the faded denim jacket of the flag holder. He raised the flag, red as fresh blood, as if marching at the point of three infantry divisions. The bell rang.

Lullabye Keed bolted out of the gate in one perfectly timed lunge. Turning Lady, #4, went out after her. The leader cut to the inside and the field bunched in behind her. Turning Lady was a nose in front of Wake Up, and Sylvia's Secret was a length behind them waiting for the leaders to spread out at the turn. They would be wide on the first turn because of the speed, I thought. My Girl looked good hanging onto the Secret's rump. The others were outrun as they moved close to the first turn. Dancing Down glided up to stay with My Girl. Lullabye Keed was two lengths in front at the turn.

I looked at the first-quarter time: 21.3. Fast. As expected. The next quarter would be the telling one. Anything less than 44.3 would mean that the #7 filly would likely fade at the finish. They couldn't let Pincay steal the race, so no one would let her get any farther ahead and would probably run at her early.

Wake Up headed Turning Lady, and My Girl and Sylvia's Secret were getting ready to take her, too. The announcer called Dancing Down, who decided that the time was right. Turning Lady was passed by Sylvia's Secret and My Girl on the outside in the middle of the turn. Dancing Down made a big move that carried her to the far outside on the turn and to third place behind Lullabye Keed and Wake Up. As they began to straighten out into the stretch, the totalizator board flashed 44.3 for the half. The seven filly, Lullabye Keed, could still hold on. It was fast, but she had saved ground and they still had to catch her. At the straightaway, #7 had it by a length, Wake Up was widening the distance on Dancing Down, who had been put away. Sylvia's Secret was moving. The others were out of it. Grandma tried to move. The jock gave her a good whipping, but she hung and he gave up.

The crowd began to pound its feet and its fists. Ladies screamed, "Get 'im! Get 'im! Move! You Mother Fucker!" and men shouted, "Get your ass in gear!"

Dancing Down lugged in and Sylvia's Secret flew by and up to my horse. They were head and head. Wake Up was on the inside. Number 7 had them both by a half-length at the head of the stretch. The three of them were driving and getting whipped. Each stride brought the first horse back to the other two. If she was caught she would stay caught. She couldn't come on again. Only great thoroughbreds can manage that. The jockey was careful not to bump or whip the other filly. Each head seemed to have melted into part of the horse.

Lullabye Keed left plenty of room for the two others on the rail. They were together seventy yards from the finish, but the speedster was fading by millimeters and the other two were glued together, squeezing in front. I heard myself growling, "C'mon, you bitch! C'mon, you bitch!" There was no space between them. "C'mon!" Their noses bobbed together. Whips flew. I held my breath.

They blurred past the finish line and I had an instant sensation as to who won. The animals were split by a nose at most. It was gambler's instinct. You know a winner without a photo. You *know* when seven is your next roll. You know not to double down on pictures, but sometimes you do.

The crowd was still gasping.

"You won! You won!" Elizabeth screamed, pounding my arm with her fists. "She won. I knew it!"

I smiled and said, "Your friend's horse won."

"Number 3? What? No chance. I saw it."

"You'll see. The photo sign will come off in a minute."

I looked at the Sarafins' box. Sylvia gazed at me with

a frigid anger. I could tell she was not a born horse player, but played bigger games. I thought she was measuring me. Walter Sarafin leaned toward her and murmured something easily. She didn't respond. He rose and tugged at her gently. She did not stop looking at me.

"She is not exactly happy at this moment," Elizabeth said. "But that sonofabitch Walter is always the same. He never breathes hard."

"Except——."

She pulled away. "I never asked you if your lady friends scream or moan or lie silently in prayerful repose while you plug away, did I?"

"No. And don't."

We fell silent, waiting.

The PHOTO sign flicked off.

Number 3 was posted as the winner with #6 and #7 second and third.

Sylvia's face gleamed with a vengeful triumph. I gave her a nod, an adversary electricity flowing between us. She had to win, no matter what. So did I. It struck me as obsessive and sad at the same time. Her lips formed a silent "Meet me later."

I stuffed my tickets into Elizabeth's hands while she tried to twist away and shut Sylvia's mouth. "Stay away from her, Harvey—or else!"

———————◆———————

Llewelyn Mackin was waiting for us in the bar. I took the seat next to him and motioned at Elizabeth to sit next to me.

"You win some, you lose some," he said.

"I prefer winning."

He leaned around me. "Miss Hume, would you join Sergeant Oliver on the patio please? You can't miss him.

He smokes cigars and wears jackets that look like Horse Blanket Billy's."

He turned to me. Large folds under his eyes signaled weariness. But it wasn't lack of sleep. "Don't look at me like I'm ready to croak, Harvey. I'm not. I'm just ready to settle down and wonder when the phone will ring."

I ordered a tall Virgin Mary. Charlie didn't look at me when he put it down.

"You know, Harv, I want to get that man out there. He's got a big shipment coming in . . . everything. You name it. It's in the millions. But no one has even gotten close to him."

"He's just smarter than cops."

"Probably. He's smarter than the bureaucracies, that's for sure. You know you probably lost two months' worth of my pension in exactly one minute, nine and three-tenths seconds?"

"Does that bother you?"

"Sometimes."

"It bothers me, too. Not for my sake, because I like winning and I like the money. There were plenty of years when I cooked rice and opened cans of corned beef hash. It bothers me for your sake."

He coughed and laughed at the same time, his cheeks jiggling like warm jello. "That's hardly serious. I don't need anything. Make a good living. Really don't need much. I want to get married and have someone clean up behind me—and not resent it—you know. And I want to get Walter Sarafin as a last gesture to my job and too . . . my own sense of well-being. I'm almost finished. A hundred more days. It's been my security blanket. I could stay, you know. I don't *have* to retire. I just *need* to retire from all of this." He pointed at my pistol and then his own. "Anyway, I've got it all figured out."

I said, "But I'm not like you. I want to keep going. There's nothing else in the world for me but getting

involved in all the lives around. It's like crossing wires."
I sipped my drink. "You know about my run-in with
Tony, and William Antonnini is still out there, waiting."

"Harvey, I repeat: I need to get Sarafin and company.
You can make it possible."

"I don't have a bunch of terrific alternatives right now.
So naturally I'll help you, then her, then Henry, then
Tony, and somewhere down the line maybe me."

The lines for the Exacta race began to extend themselves. Fistfuls of money and tout sheets, cigarette smoke
and nerves, stuffed into one great clanging room. You
could put it to music. I strode out to the patio, saw
Elizabeth with Sergeant Oliver and sat at an empty table
nearby.

Mackin followed and persisted. "Harv, I told Captain
Lopes that you'd help. It's a matter of honor now."

"Honor? Mack, deal with me on the basis of you and
me, or on the basis of me getting involved on the official
side of the law, but don't spout too much of that honor
crap because it just gets me an upset stomach. I don't
like the idea of getting killed or killing for the sake of
'honor.' That's for kids."

We were silent. I suppose I was the only one other
than Julia that he could talk to—and maybe I was the
only one because we were from the old school and we
didn't talk to wives and sweethearts.

"Still," he said, quietly, "you have to understand. It is
a matter of how I end this portion of my life. I don't
mean 'end' . . ." he was groping. "I mean 'end' and 'beginning' and how I live the beginning. I would like to
think . . ." he stopped and sighed. "Screw it. It's all in
here." He smiled almost sweetly and tapped his forehead.

"All right," I said. "Sarafin wants me to protect him
because someone is after him. We both think it's the same
someone. Sylvia keeps giving me high signs. Acts the part
of a secret confidant."

"Playing a role."

"Could be. But it wasn't her shooting at me. It was certainly William. Everything fits. Him and Mary. Together. God, *Mary*. I can't get rid of her."

"Still?"

"Still," I repeated. "And that's where she'll stay until this is over."

"She was just a——"

"Don't say it, Lew."

Mackin leaned forward. "OK, I won't. But she *was* just a pawn." He needed a shave. It was 5 p.m. and he always needed a shave by 5 p.m. "I need to stop Sarafin, Harv. I need to."

"Lew, I don't have a chance of getting to the exact time and place of this landing if I trip over you everywhere I turn." I saw Elizabeth coming toward us. "If I can get my hands on Hank Selmon, maybe I can be there when they land the plane."

"And then?"

I pulled Elizabeth into our *tête-à-tête*. "Then maybe I'll let you in on it. Maybe."

"Sounds ominous," she smiled.

"Not so," I said. Llewelyn smiled and nodded at me. "She's the one, huh?"

"What does he mean by that, Harvey?"

"He means, you are the girl of my dreams—I think. Or he could mean, are you the girl who is always where you shouldn't be?"

"I should be with you, and that's where I am." She put her hand on my chest and her arm around my waist. "Is there such a thing as a normal life for a gambler, lieutenant?" I detected a thickness in her words. She had not been drinking.

"No. Harvey has never lived a normal moment. Just degrees of insanity."

"He'll change," she said. "I'll lure him into lecturing or book writing or something quiet like that."

"How will you do it?" I asked.

"With sex. I won't let you up for air."

Llewelyn Mackin laughed from his belly.

"I still want a good answer to my question," I said. "Here, give me your purse." I pulled it quickly from her left hand.

"Stop that," she said. "What was that for?"

"It's an old license that detectives have," Mackin said.

"What happened to your pistol, dear?" I asked sweetly, after a quick look in the purse.

"I don't have one."

Leon, the maître d', approached. He crooked his index finger at me. Mackin started to move with me but I squeezed his elbow lightly and he stopped. I told Leon to wait.

Turning to Lew Mackin, I said, "I'll be in touch with you in a few hours, Mack. Just a few."

"Call this number." He handed over a cardboard slip. "It'll get you patched through to me wherever I am. I'll be close no matter what. Watch yourself. Carefully."

"I always do."

"Harvey," Elizabeth said, "this whole business is dumb. Why don't you quit? Just quit?"

"Why don't *you*?"

───────────◆───────────

I ran down to the parking lot. Sasha pointed at a maroon Porsche stuck between cars. Henry Selmon was inside screaming at an attendant to get him out of the middle of the trap. He had started to babble with frustration. He paid no attention to me as I looked into his eyes. They were dilated. He was on cocaine again. Or on something.

In spite of my reservations about her condition, I sent Elizabeth home, telling her that I would have Nails or Billy call her. Then I leaned close to Selmon. "You're not getting out, Hank. Unless it's with me."

"Get me outta here. Out! Out!"

"Henry," I said, evenly, trying to cool him. "I'll help you. You need me. You've got to trust me."

"Yes, I can trust you . . . that's right . . . yes." He stared absently for a moment. Then he nodded and smiled. "That's right." Perhaps the dawn had come.

"OK. Come with me. I can get out right now. You can leave the Porsche here. Sasha will watch it. He'll keep the keys overnight."

I motioned to Sasha, then reached in and we both helped Hank to my car.

27

Selmon was out by the time I got him safely home. At least I hoped he was safely on ice for a while. I went home, too, and waited. As I did so, in the darkness, the hair on the back of my hands stiffened. Reflections from the wet sky bounced around the black cavern of my home. Silhouettes jumped at me.

I tried reviewing my information files. I had reached a blank. It was all too close. Shutting the intensity lamp made my eyes take their time in adjusting to the dark.

I could have predicted the entrance. It would not be from the ocean side. I might kill someone approaching from that direction. He would be quick. Lugubrious and quick. Everything calculated to be unexpected.

Coming up as he did, in an institutional environment, it was surprising how urbane a man he was. In the middle of his "hang the bastards" exterior, there had always been a touch of gentle humanity, and, as in all such vulnerable creatures who have lost the narrowness of single-minded vision, there was a streak of ambition.

So when I reflected on my conversations with Llewelyn, my mind constructed the next series of events rather easily.

I sat on the red-tile steps that descended into my living room, in the waiting dark, fully convinced that wisdom dictated a retreat, but perversely glued to what was to be.

The living room door latch turned in a ghostly way. Of course, instead of through a window or a smashed glass pane, he entered through the normal entrance. I did not think his pistol would be out. I reached for my flashlight and held it away from my body. There was only my own breathing as the door opened. A little three-in-one oil and my own goddamn key did the trick.

I flicked the switch on and the beam caught him directly in the eyes.

"Please don't move, Lew."

He froze . . . because he knew it was me and remembered. "We're not going to have a scene," I said. "We've each been around too long. Friendship is an interesting status, Lew. That's all."

"I know what it is, Harvey. After all, you and I invented betrayal, didn't we? We *are* the original sin. We decided that duty was all that existed. Everything became easy after that."

"Just tell me when you got a key?" I asked.

His eyes crinkled. "Long time ago, Harvey. I couldn't let you go without police protection."

"How?"

"We can get into anything, anywhere, anytime . . . ."

"Are you going to try to put me away?"

"One way or another," he said, with a heavy sigh, pistol in hand.

"Well, come on in. I can't turn on the lights for you."

"I know. Is he always out there?"

"Probably . . . I can feel him now—out there in the sand. Let him do it for you."

Mackin hitched up his trousers. They were long on him because they buttoned under his belly instead of around it. His sleeves were long, and the blue grey plaid of the suit had faded into a uniform-like dull surface. He said nothing, no response. We stared at one another.

Finally, I said, "You look like a lost Saint Bernard. I feel like rumpling your hair and telling you to go lie down in a cool corner." All at once I was back in control.

"There's always one more game left in an old dog. At least till he's buried."

"And the old dog in you has got something cooking."

He nodded abstractly. "Just like when you left the service, 'member that?"

"Um. You wanted to hire a regiment for me to locate."

"I think it was a division."

"Well, I'm not doing very well at the locating business anymore."

He closed the door noiselessly and sat down next to me. I shut the flash.

"Put your piece down," I said.

He placed it on the cold tile. "I always wanted to quit anyway. I didn't want to even think about getting shot or clubbed or getting dumped into the Paris sewage system. Just wanted to quit. Quitting became my obsession. Quitting *is* my obsession. But not quitting and rolling my tent into a two-bit pension. No sir."

"And now you've figured out a way."

Suddenly I knew. And shook my finger at Llewelyn. "You. You and Sam . . . working together . . . but not for the LAPD. Not the Blue Knights." It hit me. I almost laughed. I waited. I could see his face as if under a microscope. It didn't move. He said, quietly "Too bad," and I said, "What does 'too bad' mean?"

"It means whatever is necessary."

"You would take me out, wouldn't you?—deprive me of going to Sam's funeral and have to join him instead?"

"Exactly, Harvey Ace, my friend. Exactly. I'm not ready for you to get in my way." His face settled into a Buddha's countenance. "It all depends on you, Harv. I'm ready for one single thing: my salvation. It's all out there in the desert. Waiting for me." He turned angry suddenly. "I can do what I want with your life now, Harvey." He ran his hand across his forehead then down over his nose, and sniffed. "That's a fact."

It was clear now. Sam Rosenstock had come across the edges of the transaction. Mackin and Sam met when Sam called in the LAPD. They concocted their parting gift to straight society. Meanwhile, Sam kept uncovering little pieces of the story that overlaid everyone's plans—the story of Henry and Tony and Walter and Sylvia, and Mary Jarn, and he came to believe that a variety of double crosses were being hatched. "And it all came down to you, Harvey. Sam always thought that Harvey Ace had an ace in the hole."

"Which explains, I guess, why he wasn't keen on helping me."

"Harvey, you and I could handle the whole thing . . . we could . . . ."

I told him to stop, and he leaned back and pulled at his cheeks. "I don't know if Sam would have made it anyway. He probably would have gotten killed," he reflected. "Billy just simplified things by getting into the middle."

"You betrayed Sam, didn't you? You set him up. Just a word or two to get him to try to take on William Antonnini."

A wave of anxiety swept over me, like the phosphorescent waves at the edge of the ocean.

"It wasn't that way. It was a mistake. A terrible mistake. He kept digging deeper into it."

"And now me?" I rose and waved my hand. "There's nothing you can do to me, Lew. You've lost control, or you wouldn't be here. That's the real fact. There's only one answer for you . . . get out while the gettin' is good. Or get it over with now. That's why you're here. Take me and blame William. Set that psycho up. Kill all birds with one stone."

"Sorry, Harv."

This hulk of a cop had mislaid his morality. There was no use arguing with him. But I tried.

"You know that I have my own concerns in this affair, Lew." I stood up and pointed into the western blackness. "I'm sure William is out there now, ready to bust me open with a .30 caliber slug. I'm sure that you turned the key in his head. Maybe Walter, maybe Sylvia. But it's really you. Mary Jarn is dead, Cyril Weber is dead. Michael Jarn. Those people—the Sarafins, they feed on dying souls and you're serving your guts up to them—and Sam was. You serve the purposes of the corrupt and they laugh. They don't give a damn, Llewelyn. For god sakes, they don't give a damn. They have corporate morality. They hide behind their own advertisements."

He smiled distantly. "You're not getting through. I've lived without caring much about me and what all the tomorrows would be. When I made love, I made love—I wasn't *in* love. And now there's two sides. Retire and live on a pension and let Julia work while I take occasional night-watchman jobs and consider myself a fool, or do what I intend to do and get out clean and learn about the good life. Everyone wants a shot at the good life."

"You're a fool."

A thin moon began to illuminate the beach in a blue phosphorescent glow.

"Umm, but I'm the expert, Harvey." He reached for his pistol. "Perhaps I am a fool, a lifetime fool with baggy pants and a steady job that might kill me at any moment. I can't take that kind of foolishness anymore. Anyway, where is it written that you're right and I'm wrong?" He rose. "Besides, the corrupt are not corruptible. It's a state of being. So you will assist and not make trouble? And recognize weakness of the flesh—and soul—and not make trouble?"

"No. You might as well shoot now."

He placed the business end of his pistol on my temple. His face grew red.

"OK. OK, Harvey," he intoned softly. "Maybe not now. Maybe we're just a couple of old army buddies gone crazy. But, I mean it, Harv. Don't get in my way."

28

———— ◆ ————

At dawn there was a tap tap tapping at the glass door on the ocean side of my flat. The creases around Elizabeth's eyes were like sharp cuts on a child's face. Her eyes avoided mine, but I could see in the early light that they were full and black and frightened.

She stumbled in and groaned and tried to pull me down to her on the couch. I held back.

She said, "I'm in a lotta trouble, Harvey."

I wondered where the lovely side of life went. "So'm I, kid. Lots . . . talk to me. Talk to me."

"Yeah, there's nothing left." She wiped her eyes with the back of her left hand and I saw the marks. Small, new scales. "Oh, god, Harv. I don't know where to start."

"Just once over lightly, once over very lightly, Elizabeth."

"I fooled you. It was easy, really. It began with a little upper now and then. A little downer about midnight. Protein drink in the morning with an upper. Off to work. Another upper. A week of that and then a weekend of just downers, Quaalude, Valium, reds. Just sleep for a whole weekend. Then get yourself on an upper again. It's really great—really . . . except, sometimes I got hungry." She laughed and sobbed. "You can't really appreciate it until you've had three days flat on your back with a little juice and a protein malted. There's nothing, jus nothing to think about. No worries. Really." She shook her head. "It's not terrible——"

"Until——"

"Until you get strung out. You can't do anything about it. Or you need too many downers and then too many uppers. If you could only keep control, it would——"

"And you almost manage to keep control."

"I fooled you. Most of the time."

I sat up on the couch and held her hands. They crawled around within my grasp.

"I didn't do anything for him, Harvey. I did him favors. You know, drops and errands and things. My life was all orderly. I had school, he provided the pills and then the heroin. Sometimes I had you. The price was right."

"Everyone's price is different."

"Yours is different, Harvey. Solitude and scrubbed hands and more solitude. Solitude, the track and occasional sex. The modern man." She started to laugh. "Maybe not *different* at all. Maybe typical—the closer you are, the further you've got to be."

"We're not on my case——"

"That's where you're wrong." She put her cheek next to mine. Her breath was warm, spreading around my ear in irregular bursts. "We are on your case. We've been on your case all along. I've been reporting on you, Harvey. Walter wanted to know what *you* were doing. Not Henry or Antonnini or anyone else. Just you."

I pushed her away slightly. "Are you in control now?"

"For a change. I don't know for how long, though. And I'm broke."

"Get your money from him. Not me."

"Please, Harvey. I need money. I can't go back to him. I won't last a month." She agreed to "reform"—stay off drugs, all at the Westside Clinic. I didn't believe her but handed her a couple hundred. She smiled one of those fleeting, thin smiles that mean other things.

"She said, 'I saw one of your best friends meet Sylvia at a Denny's in Newport. It was just yesterday. They smiled and tried to act ordinary. You could tell they were trying.'"

"You mean Lieutenant Mackin?"

"No, Harvey. I hardly ever saw him. Not regularly, anyway."

"Tony Antonnini?"

"Yes. Tony and Sylvia."

"What's your price now, Elizabeth?"

"My price is you. I want you. What's your price?"

She bothered me. She kept cutting through the outer layers. I rose. "My price is peace and quiet, and seeing if I can keep a lot of people from getting killed."

Her hands fluttered on her lap. "That's not a price, Harvey. It's a pious proclamation." She rose unsteadily and went into the kitchen and poured cold milk, and rolled a swallow around her throat before downing it. "What's your price?"

For some reason I wanted to say the word *love* but couldn't.

"You fool!" She stiffened into a sudden storm. "You're going to be dead soon and I can't stand it—wanting you and knowing what's going to happen! Oh, god, Harvey. Just get out. Please . . . go away!"

29

———◆———

Traffic eased its way circumspectly along Interstate 5. I dialed and cradled the car phone on my shoulder while Selmon drifted into the arms of his special Morpheus.

Solly the "Show Horse" answered with a whispered, "Yeah, whadaya need?"

I told him who it was and asked him about market conditions. We spoke as two stock brokers might—and probably do.

He told me that the street price for everything was high. Too high. He said that his man 'outta San Peedro says they're gettin' the best prices now 'cause the whole market goes to hell in a week. Says he c'n get me anythin', anythin' I want—cheap. Real good prices. All the distributors got calls. It's comin'. Next week. But don't call me, I'll call you."

I asked him why he didn't stick with bookmaking. And he asked me if I was crazy: "The money in this shit is unreal. I'm up to my ass in money. I don't know what to do with it. Listen, I don't make the hopheads, they make themselves. I ain't guilty a nothin'."

Then I called a bookmaker who ran a little grocery store in East L.A. and asked him what the action on the street was. "The whole world knows what's going," he said. "I gotta have my cash ready, Ace, or I get shut out. I gotta pay for a lotta shit or I get shut out. I gotta take my, you know, my prorated share. You gotta take your share or no deal. They ain't kiddin' either. These people gotta lock on lullaby land. No shit, Ace. Just plain no shit. Everybody's got to be real careful and step on no one's shoes or . . . bang, bang. You dead, bro'. They call up and they say Taurus and you gotta jump."

"Don't do it," I said. "Don't do it."

"You crazy?" and the phone went dead.

I called Lew. "I've got Henry with me. He's leading me to it. What about William Antonnini? You pick him up yet? Or, you letting him wander out there looking for me?"

"We're handling it."

"I'm gonna be there with bells on."

"You wanna get in the dead way, that's fine. Go right the hell ahead . . . asshole."

Hank Selmon stirred from his highway-induced doze. Ten years ago Sylvia had clung to him with possessory absoluteness, barely able to catch her wind as they posed for a hundred pictures in a dozen winner's circles, as they dined at Chasen's and Jimmy's and went to charity balls with Bob Hope and Fred Astaire and jocks and rich and fancy owners and then smoked hash and tried out a little of that innocent coke stuff.

He must have been in that dream when he smiled as he straightened up. "Stay on the 405. Then take the 99 after the Grapevine and let her rip. I'll tell you when to cut off."

"It'll get dark soon," I murmured.

"So much the better."

"How much time do we have?"

"Plenty."

"Is Elizabeth in on this?"

"She's not in on anything."

Selmon told me that he and Tony had made final arrangements earlier that day. I asked him if Tony knew about Sam Rosenstock. He didn't answer. He said they were told to go to the rendezvous in their own cars and that was why he was going along with me. Not to mention I might kill him if he didn't.

"Who told you the date and time?"

"A fuckin' birdie. A big one. I know and you know. So don't ask anymore."

They were told that their payoffs would be made first. Tony had his entire stash of $800,000 with him. The plane would dump out their shares and take the money. Then they were to get out of there—fast. The airplane's engines would not stop until that transaction was over. He and Tony were a team. They had a motel room in Bakersfield and a distributor meeting them at the Chevron station at Highway 99 and the Central Avenue off ramp. They were going to be handed four million dollars. He said, "four fucking million dollars!——just like that. Like it was nothing."

He told me the kind of airplane, the precise nature of the inventory being delivered, the way they communicated. Tony created the communications system based on a chess board; Baghdad DS to Knights 5. Baghdad was a tiny coffee stop near the landing strip. DS was Deep Springs, another dot on the map that determined the direction. There was a chess code for the time and location. It was near Blackwater, east of Red Mountain and China Lake. Everything was perfect, except no one could have found the small area of the landing strip without having been there before. That part was left to the memory only.

I reminded him that William Antonnini was still out there after me. "The kid thinks I had something to do with Mary's death, that I'm part of this entire scheme. Sarafin must have done a very good job on him. Sam put it all together somehow. And now poor old Sammy is dead."

Selmon's fists were clinched. He let go and then clinched, again and again. He needed his high.

"Now you know why getting high is the only way." He spoke bitterly. "I've been high and low. High is better. Just keep going, Harvey. And stop talking. I'm not on the junk right now. Thirty-six hours clean."

"A detour first," I said.

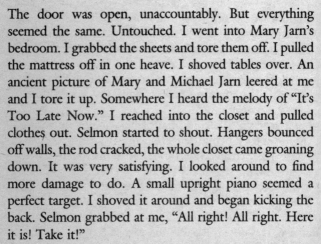

The door was open, unaccountably. But everything seemed the same. Untouched. I went into Mary Jarn's bedroom. I grabbed the sheets and tore them off. I pulled the mattress off in one heave. I shoved tables over. An ancient picture of Mary and Michael Jarn leered at me and I tore it up. Somewhere I heard the melody of "It's Too Late Now." I reached into the closet and pulled clothes out. Selmon started to shout. Hangers bounced off walls, the rod cracked, the whole closet came groaning down. It was very satisfying. I looked around to find more damage to do. A small upright piano seemed a perfect target. I shoved it around and began kicking the back. Selmon grabbed at me, "All right! All right. Here it is! Take it!"

He opened the bottom of the piano, down near the pedals. "Here it is. Tons of money!"

I opened a brown legal-size valise. He was right. Tons of money. I laughed.

"Harvey, she was not what you think. She was——"

I raised my hand. He shrugged. I didn't want to hear any more.

When we were on our way again, Selmon said, "You're as crazy as the rest of us."

I opened the window of the car and began letting fistfuls of money fly into the wind. Selmon kept trying to grab my arm but it did no good. I kept dumping money out onto Ventura Boulevard, somewhere near Tarzana just before you get to the on ramp to the 405 North.

30

<hr />

Remembering that morality was for playwrights, I toyed with the notion of using Henry Selmon to take out Lew Mackin. A double double cross. Then the money would be mine, mine and theirs. And I would be in the middle of it . . . unless, unless Sarafin and company were also removed.

"We should get there very early, Ace," Selmon said, eyeing me as if he were sitting on a ledge on the inside of my forehead watching the wheels turn. "That is, if you have any special plans. I don't know what's in there, but it's gotta be something."

"Let's just get this thing over with . . . alive."

The road wound, like a fat black snake, up into the starry night, stars closer than the horizon, and the distances beyond them too far for the mind's eye to imagine. Trucks strained toward the top, digging into the cement as if leaning into the wind, knowing that easy times would come, down the steep grade to the hot San Joaquin Valley from 5,000 feet to 500 feet in a quick whisper.

"All I really want you for," I told Selmon as I pushed the Jag into the climb, "—is to show me the exact spot. Other than that, stay out of the way. Do what you need to do and stay out of the way."

"That cop friend of yours might already be there."

"Maybe."

Once down on the flat we left traffic behind, and once off the freeway the traffic thinned to an occasional car which glared at us until past. My stomach began churning.

"Hank, I don't think there will be anything resembling a cop around except Llewelyn Mackin. Mackin wants to knock off the whole deposit—for his retirement fund, sort of like collecting the proceeds of a profit-sharing plan he's been building up to all his life . . . ."

After a moment he released his tension with a laugh. "I remember the last time we played with Walter——"

"He got *very* angry——"

"And people were shooting at people and everybody was going crazy——"

"I'm angry too."

"For all the wrong reasons." His voice was a thin whisper.

"*I* have a problem and I'm trying to make the best of it."

He lit a cigarette. The flash of the lighter illuminated his squinting eyes. I opened his window an inch or two.

"It always costs me to 'go along.' " he said, "I'm like a fucking moth. I can't say no when a light goes on."

"You mean you just can't say 'no' to all that money."

He mused a while, smoke drifting into the dashboard glow. "I suppose I'm just defective in that department. I lost my off switches. That's all."

There were no lights anymore, no counterpoint to the hum of the car on its way deeper into the desert. We were hitting a steady ninety miles per hour.

"Just remember, Harvey, Tony and I get ours and we get outta there. Fast. You got it?"

I didn't reply.

After a while he asked, "You ever sleep on the desert at night?"

"Yes," I said, wondering.

"It gets cold. Very cold."

"I remember."

"That's how I feel now. I know that Mackin fellow has got money in his gut. Just like me. That's all he can see now. That's all—he can think in hell. He ain't no player. He's just a onetime killing machine."

31

———◆———

The hard edges of distant hills were lit gently by starlight. We curled down into a shallow valley. You had to be within a couple of miles of the spot to see it from the highway. Well chosen.

We left the roadway and crunched over the thin veneer of sand covering hard packed ground. I wheeled the Jag around and repeated the route. "I think we ought to cover this whole valley," I said.

"You can see the whole damn thing from here."

"You don't know Mackin. He could hide his tonnage behind a three-inch yucca if he had to, and there are plenty of those here."

I kept the car in low and covered the run of the area, straining to see if there was a storage shed at the northwest end of the field. It was 10 P.M. Midnight was the time. I felt Llewelyn's presence but pushed it away. There was time. Then I aimed in the direction of the highway and flipped off the lights.

We found the shed and Henry went to it and took candles and bags and, just like Halloween pranksters, created a landing field with desert sand anchoring the flickering candles in the bags. I doubted if they could be seen from higher than 4,000 or 5,000 feet, but the markers would glow like golden sapphires to a pilot who was looking for a landing spot in the empty darkness.

"Remember," he said, "we load up Tony's pickup and get the hell out." I heard dried mesquite crack. At that instant I knew I wasn't ready for the encounter. A walnut of hollowness in my stomach grew. And I was aware that I always felt the same when stalking and being stalked. You wanted to be somewhere else—far, far away—you felt like giggling when you realized that you were never more than a moment or two from teatime with death. Certain chromosome compounds in some people kept them glued to the time and place of death. I followed the noise, expecting attack. I was convinced my every move could be heard for a mile.

❖

Henry said, "No one here—it's too early. Besides, Mackin will probably bring an army and try to hide them in tanks along the road. That's how they all work, you know."

"I'm certain he's here—unless jackrabbits make a lotta noise."

"They do. They're noisy fucks. Like me."

We had used forty candles in making an approximate half-mile strip. Selmon followed me away from the light. He shivered once as we sat on the desert floor. In a while I was conscious of the aliveness of the desert. Lizards scurried in and out, as if checking the angle of starlight, and made tiny whispers in the sand, as did the hunting of sharp-toothed rodents and snakes, each hunting the other. From nowhere, breezes brushed over us. And then stopped. And it was hushed. I stopped breathing and listened.

❖

"Hello, Llewelyn," I said into the darkness.

Selmon turned, eyes wide. "Wha——?"

"Relax, Henry," Mackin said, invisibly. He hustled in next to us. "You're all set, huh?"

"I just set it up like good old Henry here said it's supposed to be. I thought you would get things going."

As he stood above us, light from the bagged candles yellowed his baggy face.

"I suppose the rest of your brothers will be setting up soon," Henry said, as if I had never spoken to him.

"No, Henry. Just keep your questions for the time being," I replied. "We might have to change our plans."

"Probably," Lew replied flatly.

"Exactly."

"I hope you guys know what the hell you're doing," Selmon said. "We're going to have a private army on us. Two guards at least, three loading hands on the plane, and the pilot. Plus the regulars: Tony, Walter, Sylvia, and whoever else they spring on us."

"We've already counted. You don't have to deal with everyone. Just parts of the whole. You'll see," I said. "Cut the fingers and the arm is useless; cut the foot and the leg is useless. You'll see." I turned to Mackin. "Where is your car?"

"The other side of the highway."

I made mental notes where all the players should be when Mackin made his move . . . some by the car, some by the plane and some by the truck. And I tried to sort each spot out for each player. I closed my eyes. There was a soft coherence of sound around me so that lost events came to mind and reminded me that only man had lost his coherence, his predictability. Mackin could not predict or control the night. He thought he could, but he was wrong. I could not. The events to come, once launched, would take on their own separate existence and the play would go its way irrespective of our pleadings, our prayers, or our guns. "You better get going, Llewelyn. Tony and Hank have their own scenario. Let them finish. We'll have enough trouble without getting careless."

Even with my eyes closed, I could clearly see his heavy face nod lugubriously and his eyelids narrow the orbits of his eyes. "Listen," I added, "I want Sylvia Sarafin alive no matter what." I was looking at him now. "Alive, Llewelyn . . . No matter what."

He threw a silent OK at me and faded into the dark.

It was dawning on him that each of us had our own agenda. From the darkness I heard, "I don't like this at all."

Hank said, "This ain't gonna go well. Not with you guys around. I know it."

"It's inevitable, Hank. You and Tony and the rest started it years ago, and it grew—like Topsy—and no one could have stopped it. Maybe it will lend some meaning to Mary's death, and Sam's too. God knows, there's no sense in it now."

"But there's gonna be dead bodies out here if you don't get the hell out. You and Lew. I don't understand you you're fucked. That's what. Totally fucked."

"I told you what was going to happen right from the start. I told you. But you didn't believe me. You should have. Reality was when you made your bargains with Sarafin and Tony and Lew, and dope and whoever or whatever else your soul made deals with. Don't bitch now, 'cause here we are." There was a quiet time. Then "C'mon. We're going to come out of this—I've got it all worked out. Take one of the flare guns and load it. I'm just here to see to it that some people come out alive— you and Sylvia and Tony and Lew. Now get that damn flare gun and load it up."

He obeyed.

32

———◆———

A yellow cold half-moon drifted into the western sky and mixed with the night, turning the desert a creamy blue. Everything was touchable. Now I could reach the stars.

Headlights bothered the stillness. As they approached, they seemed to grow tentative. This was the spot, all right, I thought.

"I told you," Hank said.

The limo pulled up to within thirty yards, and the lights went off. Nothing happened.

"Just remember—bounce the flare off the car when I give the word."

Minutes passed. Walter was being appropriately cautious. The back door opened and a flash beam reached out at us at the same time as the thud of the slammed door.

Shading my eyes, I could see Walter and Sylvia. They kept their distance. I waved. No one moved.

"To hell with them. We'll stay here. Llewelyn is out there somewhere, anyway."

After counting 100 breaths, two half-ton trucks rumbled off the road. Each were side-loading vans. They parked thirty yards in the opposite direction and thirty yards from each other, lights off. A small panel truck approached, and Antonnini emerged with another smallish man who had a hand in his hip pocket and who stood at the door as Tony glided toward us.

Antonnini's steps on the damp rocky floor of the desert seemed to burst into the breathless quiet. He signaled in Sarafin's direction. "Shut the goddamn flash, Sarafin!" His voice sounded like sawdust being born. His heavy head swayed back and forth. "Damn him! That little sliver of light makes him think he's in control . . . Shut it!" he shouted.

It went off, and it took a minute for his eyes to adjust to the darkness. He shuffled over, shoulders hunched as if ready to jab. His driver followed.

"Don't know why you're here, Ace. No reason for it. None. None at all."

"You're seven years too late with your advice. Seven goddamn years too late, Tony. You set me up. You dragged my ass into this insanity. You——"

"If I could do everything over again, I'd probably make bigger mistakes. We haven't got time for regrets, for any past sins. It's all shit anyway. You know that." He waved at Selmon with a right index finger.

"Let's just do what we have to, Tony," Selmon hissed.

"It might not work out like that."

"Nothing?"

Tony's eyes blazed. "Forget it. Let's go," he snapped. "Walter and company is waiting. The plane will be here soon."

Seven of us met adjacent to the middle of the landing strip. Sylvia's cigarette shone its red glow on her anxiety. She was covered with a midnight satin trench coat. Folds of her white blouse were exposed. Walter seemed self-assured—too calm. Almost nonchalant. His silver hair crowned him luxuriously.

"This is your biggest and best trade, isn't it?" I said to him.

"It could be a nice night's work."

A third guard climbed out of the limo.

"We'll have to count the money, Walter. In fact, we're doing everything differently."

"How's that?"

"Relax, dear," Sylvia murmured, letting the carcass of her cigarette drop and die.

Tony said, "We count everything *now*. Then I let the plane land."

"I have to check the load, Tony. No nonsense. It has to be inventoried."

"I thought we just took our load and got out!" Selmon whined.

"Shut up," Tony hissed. "After we count. The plane lands and stays at the far end of the field. You and I and one of your mathematical geniuses will walk over," he said to Sarafin, "do the inventory and make our trade. My end is boxed and packed separately. I take that off. Harvey and Selmon will take care of this end."

Walter hesitated. I thought I heard the drone of piston engines deep into the now-cold night. "How are we going to unload?"

"There are two loaders on the plane," Tony said, "and guns, too. So no crazy stuff. It won't take more than a half-hour to get the shit out of the plane. I'll give you the keys to the trucks when we've made our exchange."

Hank Selmon looked bewildered and lost. It was going too fast for him. And he had to obey.

Sarafin looked at his wife. "He doesn't sound like a punchy bum now, does he, dear?"

"He never was, Walter. I've told you over and over."

"This detective fellow you keep staring at. He's part of it. Aren't you, Ace?"

"At this moment, yes. For my reasons. Perhaps for your reasons. But you're wrong about the past. Good old Tony here handled everything. Used his organizational genius on you and Hank and me, and made it all work for him."

Antonnini stepped back. "Now is not the time to start praising Caesar, Harvey. This is not the place. So just keep your mouth shut."

I could feel Hank's hand slide into his coat. I smiled. "Just wanted you to know where I am."

"I think you liked me when I drank and mooched off you. When I was dependent . . . so to speak."

"That's Sam's phrase."

"You're right. It was."

"Isn't someone missing here, Tony."

"Between the two of you, we may never conclude this deal," Walter interrupted. "Play on your own time. I don't see why we have to hike a half-mile to get this over with."

"That's the way it's going to be."

"With Sylvia?" he asked.

"No. Just you and me and your man. When we are done you can include Sylvia however you choose."

The engines came closer.

"They're here," Hank said, searching the sky.

"Bring the money out," Tony said. "Let's get on with this. I have a feeling that a pack of wolves is ready to pounce."

Antonnini walked with Walter. Sylvia stayed. She gazed directly at me. "I would really like to know where you fit in," she said.

"You will. Believe it, Mrs. Sarafin."

"That sounds threatening."

I moved away from Hank and she followed. "I said that sounds threatening," she repeated into the dark.

"Nonsense. Your imagination." I motioned with the flat of my hand at Hank to stay put. I wanted some distance between the good guys if anything happened. I didn't want us to get picked off too easily. Then I thought, the good guys may not be us.

◆

Seventy or eighty pounds of money sat in vinyl thirty-inch suitcases on the desert. Four of them. One of Walter's men squatted next to them, perhaps halfway between the truck and the limo—in front of us.

It took ten minutes to finger through the cases. After it was counted they came back and Tony signaled the plane.

Where they got a Curtiss Commando, I don't know. It wasn't a customary air-cargo vehicle, but it sounded well kept. Deep hum. Dark green paint. A steady draft horse look with a humped back. It bounced toward us.

Out in the darkness Llewelyn waited.

The groan of the engines diminished and then stopped, sighing a last sigh, as if never to turn over again. An invisible hand lowered a steel ladder. Walter strode briskly toward it and Tony shouted at him as if the engines were still alive, "Don't take more than ten minutes." The sound stretched out into the night.

We waited.

It was a deadly time. And a deceiving time. The players were not defined, except in their own minds. Old friends wore masks and new enemies wore masks. Money was god and winning was everything, and winning meant more than coming out on top. It meant living. It seemed to grow darker.

Walter came out of the plane, clipboard in hand, as if he just finished inventorying a warehouse of tuna cans. Several men emerged with him. The truck backed up toward the plane and the process of unloading began. Walter came toward us. "So far so good," he said.

He seemed pleased with himself. Even arrogant. Arrogance is a fool's mistake, I thought.

"Let's keep it that way," I replied.

The truck loading was finished. Tony told Walter that the trucks had to stand by and would leave only when everyone else left. Sarafin nodded. A very lean young man emerged from the plane, took a deep breath and surveyed the area. His momentary pose was like the last member of a conquering landing party. I could hardly hear the desert crunch under his feet as he approached Walter, who handed him a brown packet a little larger than a Cheerios box.

"There's a Rent-A-Car half a mile up the road," Walter told him. "The keys are in it. Go away. You know the old saying? Don't call me, I'll call you." The pilot smiled. Full of life. Full of a quarter-million dollars.

Too goddamn arrogant, I thought again. Sarafin even moved as if he owned Western Civilization. His whole manner was as if this were a game, another horse race. It meant trouble. I was right.

From the corner of my eye, I saw Sylvia's arms raise slightly. A handbag was in one hand but the other hand was inside. Everything moved very slowly while Tony and Henry watched. The young man trudged away in the darkness.

Sylvia's arms kept raising, slowly. Slow motion. I was in her line of sight but to the side. There was time. In her hurt and fear, and rising out of the damage that had been inflicted on her over the years, she was going to take revenge. And take the money. And in the process toss a wrench into the well-oiled plans of everyone in sight. As I leaped, I had an instant of pleasure in realizing that it was Walter she was after, not Tony, not me, not Henry. She had to take control, and one swift death seemed the best way. Her finger began to close on the trigger while Walter was still smiling his self-satisfied smile. My right arm came down on her wrist. The gun popped out of her hand and slithered into the dust. Antonnini turned and ripped off two shots from not more than fifteen feet away. Sylvia burst into blood in my arms. I was conscious that one of her breasts was caught in my jacket. She seemed to splatter all over me.

Henry fired the flare gun at the closest vehicle. The night lit up like downtown Vegas.

Then he began to rip off shots wildly, and dropped Walter's bodyguard as he kneeled to return the fire. The guard rose into the air and all at once sagged, lifelessly backward. Shadows wheeled over the sky. I raised my gun and pointed it at Walter, fingers wet.

Sylvia's remains lay in a grotesque huddle at my feet, her hand not far from her pistol. Was she moving? Still out to kill . . . the final double cross? Loaders scurried in all directions. In the back of my mind I could feel Mackin move closer. I kept my gun trained on Walter. Antonnini went to the briefcases and lifted one of them gingerly. The trucks began to move away—frightened drivers wanting to save their skins. Tony's man fired two rounds at each windshield and they stopped.

All I could hear was my own breath and inside a roar, "My god, the whole night is blowing up!"

Suddenly the new silence was torn apart by another rapid series of shots. Walter was lifted from the ground in a wild backward tumble by the impact of the hit. They had come from Sylvia's pistol. She rolled over, face up. I knelt next to her.

Grotesque whites and yellows flashed at us. "Cut the flare, Henry! Stamp on it!"

Tony came toward me and knelt. There was no beauty left in the formless mess of Sylvia Sarafin. She was stained red, crumpled, and barely alive. I said, "Don't say anything. Take it easy."

Her eyes closed, then opened, as if she understood. I looked at Tony. The flare went out.

Part of what sticks out in my mind, even today, in an odd pinball-machine sort of way, is Tony's eyes just before Sylvia died. They had receded into his head and, like yellow lights of the flare striking into the night, tucked themselves in under his brow as if not wanting to see, as if dying their own, separate death. The bottom parts of the pupils darted about looking for a path to peace— away from the terror, while Sylvia's eyes receded into a glassy nothingness, and Henry's eyes, who had also come toward us, became white. Anthony Antonnini's entire countenance was altered by the fact that his eyes had withdrawn into the safety of those brows and had turned oddly yellow.

Henry fell to the ground holding his head.

Sylvia's eyes stayed open after death came.

Tony lifted her into his arms and to the limousine. He kept whispering, "I thought it was *me*." He placed her body inside.

Tony's man ordered the loaders out of the plane.

Stars lowered closer to the horizon. They grew brighter. The moon was cold.

"It's all so fucking familiar," Henry said. "Jesus! It's all so crazy. Why——?"

"It's not over yet," I replied. "In fact, it's just begun."

The events seemed to fit in a preordained way.

An unseen voice said softly to us, "Just leave everything where it is. Don't look around. Just drop everything gently, and everything will be fine. I suggest you do it right now."

"No, Llewelyn," I said into the night, "this is not the way it's going to be. You can make this your final bust, but you're not going to make it our final resting place. You're not getting the money, you're not getting the trucks and you're not getting any of us killed . . . that's absolute. Unless you want to die with us."

"Harvey," Llewelyn said, patiently, his body infused with the sound of new adrenalin, "you no longer have anything to do with any of this, you're an outsider, now.

You're useless to your friend and to me, and even to Henry over there. And you're certainly no good to Sylvia and Walter. Nothing's left Harvey, just us. And Tony. Look at him. Look. All through. He died when she did. He just keeps breathing." His teeth ground together. He was right. It was Tony and Sylvia all the way.

I could not tangle with Lew. He was just too much.

I replied, "There's still a young man out there somewhere with a high-powered rifle who has me tied into this entire matter. I've got to find a way out. I can't ignore it, Llewelyn. I need us alive and well, and I'm sure the County of Los Angeles will use the money wisely after it's impounded as evidence."

"It seems clear that we've reached our parting," Lew murmured.

All at once I heard Henry say, "Son of a bitch, someone has to pay for this." He began to sob. "I want you to die as soon as possible." He was screaming. He threw himself at Tony like a small child. Even in his near catatonic state, Tony reacted, almost gently, and heisted the tiny body and threw it aside as if it were weightless.

Llewelyn lifted the briefcases and hooked two of them over one arm. He kept his distance. I waited for the bullet. Then his body heaved and lowered even further over his belt buckle.

I was wet all over with sweat and blood. Sight was blurred. I knew I was caught in the maelstrom. I couldn't seem to get unglued. Something had gone awry. I couldn't get out.

And Llewelyn was at my side, so was Mary Jarn, that lost look on her dying face, and Sylvia, the regal plotter, caught, too. Each of us caught by ourselves, by that thing that was human and weak and curious and hopeful.

"You're fucked," Lew said, "Absolutely fucked, Ace. You're the crazy one here. Greed I can understand. Sickness I can recognize. But you're absolutely crazy. . . . Stop it, give it up."

I kept moving toward him, pointing my pistol right at his face.

"Give it up, Harvey."

I couldn't stop.

33

◆

Anthony Antonnini was found wandering in the desert a half-mile from what was left of the old Curtiss. I was found with a bleeding head propped up against my car. I surmised that I hadn't pulled the trigger. The trucks were ablaze. Mackin supervised law enforcement. He had done his homework. The LAPD, in conjunction with the Highway Patrol, and the local Sheriff's Department were in the process of rounding up "gang" members and looking for suspects in a "drug-related shoot-out" that occurred in the Southern California desert.

At least that's what the headlines of the *Los Angeles Times* proclaimed. Llewelyn still had the power, and no one suspected him, so I kept my mouth shut. I guessed that he had at least two valise's of money in his possession.

The problem that he appeared to have forgotten was William Antonnini. It was a mistake. And it was a mistake for him to believe that the entire affair would disappear quietly. There had to be somebody to blame for the killings other than gang members. He couldn't keep it under the rug forever. He must have known. He had been alone at the scene. Law enforcement didn't work like that.

It was like trying to predict an earthquake. In California, we know about those things and think about them. In some way the entire matter would shake loose in one thundering roar.

———————◆———————

I knew it before I opened the door. Her apartment was a shambles, violently askew.

Elizabeth lay in a twisted rag position in a corner next to her tan leather couch. Bloody handprints streaked across silk curtains and over white walls. I couldn't bring myself to step beyond the threshold. Not an inch. Later, I would learn that the police found a piece of a note, ". . . They wanted to take me alive. I wouldn't let them . . ."

The pain had become so overwhelming I couldn't feel it.

———————◆———————

You may think that I'm crazy. But I went to the races.

Horse Blanket Billy was waiting for me. He tried to tout me onto the four horse in the sixth race as I sat at my table staring into the brightness of the green infield trying to block out the decision that had to be made. He kept jabbing his finger at #4 on the racing form and pointing at the chart of its last race. Number 4 had the only speed in the race and could set its own pace, and Don Pierce would know just what fractions to use for the first half. I told him that Don was not a good jockey from the gate, but Billy insisted that the fourth post position was ideal for the horse. I shrugged and told him I wasn't betting the race. I wasn't going to bet anything that day. But I didn't want to go home. I had taken a hotel room near the track. I recalled looking at my face that morning and seeing a much more wrinkled man.

Billy asked if I had gone to Sam Rosenstock's funeral, and I told him that I hadn't but that I would pay my respects to his widow as soon as possible. He asked me about Elizabeth. I couldn't answer.

Then his freckled round face leaned close to me in a confidential manner and whispered hoarsely. "They say that you killed Walter Sarafin. It *was you*, wasn't it? I hated the sonofabitch." He giggled gleefully. "Oh I'm glad, Harvey, I'm glad. He had everyone by the balls. No more."

My field glasses were trained on the starting gate. "Billy, put $20 on your horse for Nails. I'm sure he needs it."

"Yeah, Harv, OK. Was I any help to you? He was a prick."

Number 4 did win the race. I went inside to the bar. Ordered a tonic that had no taste. Time had no taste. The soft, ocean-lovely day had no taste. The crowd, the winners' screaming, the smiles, the swearing, the paddock smells, sweat and misery . . . nothing had flavor.

Later, from my hotel room I called Llewelyn. When he answered, I said, "I can't hang onto all of this anymore, Lew. I'm not letting this die like the end of a war. No proclamations. I'm going to bring it to an end."

"I want to know something," he said, as if nothing had happened, as if the world remained exactly the same as it was three days ago. "Tell me how you knew that Sylvia was out to waste Walter."

"I didn't really. I guessed. They had a long history together. Henry and Sylvia split up because of Sylvia's fatal attraction to Tony. It had been going on for a long time. Maybe she just needed him, like an anchor line to her own reality. The problem was that Sylvia could never reconcile herself to Tony's way of living. But she didn't stop caring. He could never get into her league. In spite of his education and brains, he played the fool most of his life. It was easier for him. I gave him winners and Sylvia gave him fantasy. And William gave him immortality. Finally they concocted the idea of using Walter as a means of getting out of their respective situations.

"To tell you the truth, I think that William is Sylvia's son. They've known each other long enough. I'm not really sure, but it seems logical to me. Anyway, Sylvia couldn't settle for Antonnini's life or Hank Selmon's life so she sold out to Walter. Tony and Sylvia worked out the entire scheme, and the other night was to be the culmination of it, the culmination of a scheme that started seven years ago. I kept thinking that Sylvia simply wanted to get rid of everyone: me, Tony, Walter—me, in particular. Which was the easiest means to solve my intrusion. Then you started to pull the strings. . . ."

I paused and Llewelyn said, completing my own story, "But Tony was never really sure of her, and when she raised her gun he really didn't know who the victim was."

"Exactly," I responded. "And in that instant, that horrible instant, he simply decided that he had *no* allies and that he had *no* friends, and that the only one left was himself. And in the same instant everything went wrong and he blew Sylvia away."

There was a heavy silence.

"That explains why he's gone crazy now. He's been committed to Sands State Mental Hospital, where he's wild with self-destructive behavior. He needs a lawyer. If you can find him one, that would help. Have you seen William or heard from the boy at all?"

"No, I haven't," I said quietly, praying that the leopard would change its spots. "Listen, Lew, I can't keep holding this entire story in. You're going to have to work it out with the police department because I'm going to call it all in, pack it all up unless you get it all straight. Too many people are dead . . . gone. And it has to do with that girl who died at my feet, and Elizabeth's death, too. Walter's boys messed her up pretty badly. And you're a part of it. Part of all that sick greed and death."

"I'm not forgiving me, Harv. It's hard for me to know how I feel about anything right now. But you're not my keeper. None of this has anything to do with you. Just go away."

"Not interested," I replied. "We've got a string of dead people, and they all died for your sole advantage, didn't they? And so far as I can tell, I'm next. I might as well be. The last tie. I keep thinking you want to finish with a flourish."

"You've gotten obsessive. That's dangerous. Right and wrong was never your strong suit. Maybe it was, I don't know," he sighed. "Just don't get in my way."

"Sorry," I said. "No dice."

I could feel his body shrug. "By the way, thanks for not putting me away."

"*Por nada*. Maybe you'll do the same for me someday."

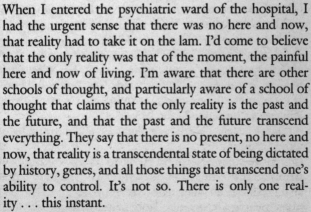

When I entered the psychiatric ward of the hospital, I had the urgent sense that there was no here and now, that reality had to take it on the lam. I'd come to believe that the only reality was that of the moment, the painful here and now of living. I'm aware that there are other schools of thought, and particularly aware of a school of thought that claims that the only reality is the past and the future, and that the past and the future transcend everything. They say that there is no present, no here and now, that reality is a transcendental state of being dictated by history, genes, and all those things that transcend one's ability to control. It's not so. There is only one reality . . . this instant.

That was the feeling I had as I was indifferently aimed toward the lonely spot where Anthony Antonnini lay in a state of emotional suspension.

Sands State Hospital was situated in a blue-collar suburb of Los Angeles south and east of downtown. It sprawled over about eight acres of yellow stucco huts and drooping eucalyptus.

A July sun had begun to heat the day.

Through the barred window, I could see patches of carefully trimmed lawn. Three narrow thrusts of palm trees angled against the smog-faded sky twenty feet to the left of the ornate wrought iron entrance to the hospital. It appeared to be the only remnant of the original structure. Eight feet of fencing topped by barbed wire imprisoned the trees and grass and sky and squat huts. Easy to get over, I thought. But it's not a prison. It's a hospital with a prison ward. Must all of the crazies be barricaded?

The pungent aroma of Lysol drifted around the corridors. Shiny black and white asphalt tile mirrored the peep holes in the doors of each room.

"This way, please. Right here. Right. Yes, that's it."

The pink attendant had gotten used to dealing with the inmates. He forgot what it was like outside. His pink round face had a pasted-on smile. "You'll find him just there. There, just . . . you see, one-two-three doors. . . ." Then he stared up at me, a resigned glance, cast like plaster into his forlorn face. "He was a problem. I must tell you. Some of these patients can try a person. There's a limit, you know. Some kind of relative?"

I didn't answer. Nothing I might have said would have been heard.

Tony was strapped into his bed. White walls, white sheets, white covers; ruddy, bearded face in contrast, chin at the fold of the sheet. Eyes open, breathing noisily.

The eyes rolled over to watch me. Beagle eyes. Not yellow anymore. No short circuits behind them. I waited. The room was bleakly empty except for the bed and the orange and yellow combination of blankets and sheets lay in agonized folds around him.

We didn't talk for an eternal five minutes. Finally, he

said, "They let me out of these things for about an hour this morning. Maybe again in a little while. Can't tell. Never tell you anything. Same as jail." He started to chuckle, then stopped suddenly. "Damn. If I laugh, I'm crazy. And if I don't see humor in life, I'm crazy. They gotcha comin' and goin'." The voice was the same—a near whisper.

He sighed and chuckled lightly again, then a little crazily until he abruptly stopped.

"You don't *look* crazy to me. But you sound a little crazy—"

"*They* think so. You know, they walk with me, two of them, right into the can and stand next to me while I piss. Can you beat it? I could leak all over them. They're not smart enough to think of that. No. That don't reach their dim wits."

He sounded reasonable. And demeaned. I figured if you still have enough sense to feel that kind of pain, then maybe there's still hope. "You look like a dead turkey, Tony."

"Harvey, I'm a very dangerous guy. Don't even try to tell me I'm OK. I came back from the can and I wanted to stay out in the area out there where you can walk around, and this one guard says no dice and one thing leads to another, you know. They're very touchy. You'd think I needed a doctor, or was a criminal, or somethin'."

"Tony, you are a very big criminal. Big-time. Dead people everywhere. Doesn't that register? Have you just let it go out of your head? Listen, I can tell you—stay crazy or be an accessory to at least two murders. Your salvation is that no one cared much whether Walter and Sylvia died, or lived, or anything. There doesn't seem to be anyone around to bitch about them."

His eyes grew hollow in their sockets again, drifting away from the here and now. I thought of Kavanaugh's poem:

The mark upon our face is sadness and horror in the color of our eyes. We have seen sights too dark for sunlight . . .

"Are you still with me?—I've got questions. Stick with me, Tony. You've left out one big fact. A monumental one." I hesitated, not sure if I had gotten past the film over his eyes. Beagle eyes.

"I'm gonna be very good now," he said, abstractly. "I'll be very quiet and they'll let me out of this room. Then Sylvia and I will go away. We've been wanting to go away. We'll just go away. I'll go back into training."

I wasn't sure how to respond. Touching his forehead, I could feel his mind struggling. "Sylvia is dead, Anthony. Elizabeth is dead. Walter is dead. We've been bloodied all over. It's been like a Shakespearean drama."

"And I'm Lear. Crazy Lear."

"The King. Long live the King."

"Blind Lear. Crazy Lear."

"Bill is still out there, Tony. He's been programmed to believe that I ruined your life, that I brought this all down on you."

He didn't answer. I wasn't sure if it had registered on him.

"In any event," I said, "the only ones left are you, William and Mackin. And me. Everyone else is dead."

He looked up. "You sound like my mother . . . or one of the doctors. I've got to face up to everything. That's what they tell me. Everything hurts. I hate you and it hurts. My fucking head hurts and my insides feel like I was hit by a left cross, hard. Real hard. I'm not going to remember. Why would anyone *want* to remember? They all think I'm as crazy as a bird. Oh, I know I get funny. I know I'm supposed to let it all out. But I get to shaking all over, and then my head goes. I'll tell you what I

remember. I remember Henry . . . screaming and screaming . . . and screaming."

The same hospital orderly stuck his head in the door.
"OK?" he smiled genuinely this time. I nodded.

"I remember a kid I managed," Tony said. "Fought at
the old Ocean Park Arena. He was so ugly that he thought
getting his face smashed would make it better. Told him
he couldn't fight anymore, but he got a fight on his own.
When it was over he couldn't speak straight or think
straight. His mother had to lead him away. Smiling. He
was smiling. I kept remembering him. He knew that he
was going too far. We all knew. The ref knew. But he
needed punishment—he needed punishment more than
life. Kept coming back for more. And more. And more."

I stopped him before he got beyond range.

"Tony. They'll kick me out soon. I need a few answers.
Like you and Llewelyn Mackin."

His eyes, which had been in reverie, now focused directly on me. "Yes. That's right."

I said, "You may have directed operations, but someone else let it all happen. Or set it up."

"Someone must have set it up," he repeated. A sneaky
grin crawled spider-like across his bearded skin. "Someone."

34

The H. Salt French fries were mushy by the time I got home. They were probably always mushy. But I didn't want hamburgers anymore. It was the diet of solitary people—isolated people. I didn't want to be like that anymore. I didn't want to be the same today as yesterday. I didn't want lonely murmurs ringing in my ears, ancient voices wanting to ease my solitary journey. And I knew, as we all know, that there are limits in all our journeys. So be it. I felt like crying aloud to the damp sea night, "We are all limited nincompoops! Don't try to kid me!"

The window shattered just above my head. My heart stopped. Lungs. Breath. Brains. Muscles. All stopped. Glass dusted my head. Hunks of jagged daggers fell at my feet.

When I shifted back to reality, I could follow where the bullet had traveled. From northwest low to southeast high. That meant *he* was crouched in the sand along the emptied stretches of the beach. Same M.O.—not clever, unless it succeeded.

I started thinking deliberately. I couldn't risk thinking too fast. William was out in the sand in grey sweats, hiding in the ripples and dunes. Waiting was no longer part of the game. I had to get out there into the night alive, and at the same time cut off his probable avenue of escape. I grabbed another clip, jammed it into my trousers, and slipped out of my shoes. My gun lay comfortably in my grip. Not too tight. Not too much tension, Ace. Relax. A bad thing to be in the middle of this chaos.

The asphalt in the alley felt like a cold shower floor. I ran behind the beachfront cedars northward, watching where I stepped. I could land in a pothole and break an ankle. Brittle bones, these Harvey Ace bones. I needed to get into the sand without being seen. If I could, we would be equal. I might have him one up. His rifle would be more unwieldy than my pistol. I could get off the first shot even if we stumbled onto each other.

After 150 yards I dashed to the side of one building and crouched low and studied the sand. I surveyed each area like a camera, framing each foot of it in my eye and mind. I panned ever so slowly over the territory. No sign. But he was there. If he was to escape northward I had been too quick for him to get away. And he would be curious. He could not be sure. It must be gnawing at him. No self respecting marksman could live with another hour of doubt. I had to get into the sand. This was the worst part.

Guessing that he would move toward the house, I nestled my stomach into the cement and moved over the walkway toward a stationery cement bench. I felt as if the curb 10 feet in front of me towered over my head like Hoover Dam. Good. I stayed low. He was beginning to move. I felt it. The other way, I said to myself. Go get me, William—the other way. I came to the bench and curb and raised my eyes and took another long stop-action study of the area. Then rolled into the sand and lay there, very still, listening to my breath.

He would be nearly on top of me if he were trying to get away without another shot. I had to take a chance and look again. Sand shoved into cantaloupe-size mounds kept me covered. Nothing.

Stars and the sound of waves cracking in a thump sent

from the China Sea. A hundred and fifty yards north the parking lot stretched barrenly. The lifeguard station stuck its head up; trash cans were gathered in a circle like yellow martinets near the volleyball courts. Someone had made a home for the night—one of the street people, the pensioners or kids who lived beneath the pier and who could survive on $6 a day in handouts: just enough for a joint and a meal.

I guessed that William would not attempt a getaway. He would hurry to another spot, closer, and rid himself of frustration. He was saying to himself, anxiously, "I've got to be sure."

I crawled straight toward the beach, seventy-five yards. But he would be studying the house. Outflank him, like Patton, MacArthur maybe. Out, then back. Sand adhered to everything. Teeth, eyes, eyebrows. I kept spitting and kept going. Suddenly my chin was in water. Going downhill. I turned carefully, looking back at my own home. Drew the pistol.

Yes. There he was, moving. Caterpillar-like. Butt and belly undulating. Always forward. I went straight for him, semicrawl. Closer. Straight and slow.

If either of us wanted a confrontation, one of us would die. But there was no alternative except confrontation and prayer. If I could get close enough, his cumbersome rifle would take him out of the game. Inflicting death had become a simple game—a little gin rummy—hi-lo, perhaps—or chess with pieces made of carved dynamite! And I knew that existence is by whim, life by chance, one unending string of corelated, yet unrelated chances— and death is simply one of the whims, a spot in time never known. We live, therefore we die. Isn't there anything better out there?

I was frightened, and I kept saying it, whispering it to myself.

And then I was less than fifteen yards from William.

"Goddamnit, William! Get your ass up and don't move a muscle! I'm gonna blast you! Blast you!"

In two bounds I was on him. He had barely turned. The ringing of my voice reverberated in my head. A broken bell, vibrating and shaking me to bits. Whirling, he tried to bring the rifle to bear on me. But he was hardly turned when the .45 jammed against his ear. "No more moving," I hissed. "No more, William."

I started to squeeze. His eyes wrenched open. White horrors in the deep night. Then he began to turn the rifle at me, daring. Ever so slowly, hypnotizingly, he kept the muzzle coming at me. "William! Don't make me do it!"

He smiled, almost sweetly. Blond shaggy mane falling like wisps of gold about his brightened face. He was going to do it. "Please, William."

I wanted to beg.

He knew it.

"If I have to, I'll do it."

The wind came up. Suddenly cold. The night had turned against me. I knew what to do. It had to be quick. I couldn't wrestle with him. Not that creature.

I raised up and came down very quickly with the pistol directly onto his temple. Still quick, Ace. I told myself like a triumphant kid. My knee aimed for his neck. His jaw went slack. There was enough reflexive action in his sinews to twist away and then he leaned suddenly backward and heaved into the sand like a bag of sawdust— slow motion and delayed only by youth. The rifle slipped away from his hand as did consciousness from his brain. Lights out. I knew what they meant by the phrase. I had seen a blow to the temple work like that before, causing death.

I noticed how thick his arms and shoulders were. He must have lifted poor Sammy Rosenstock into his attic burial ground with one hand. It was an awful indignity to be buried in a half-inch of ancient dust. The crazies

of the world should not end up as servants of death—
it's not fair to deal with death *and* crazies.

I was breathing hard, trying to tie his wrists behind
him with my belt. Of course, Ace, don't you remember?
You always forget that nothing is fair, and death and life
are the handmaidens of one another. Neither has a meaning without the other. Except, the indignity of it all.

Goddamn, you're heavy. I'd like to smash you now
and join the crazies. I cursed the cumbersome, limp form.
Wouldn't *treat* your remains like dirt, though.

I remembered my dad putting his right index finger to
his lips and saying, "Shhh, if you are very quiet at night,
all the boogeymen will pass you by and you'll never worry
about dying." I didn't know what the hell he was talking
about, but he seemed to really know because a dim smile
passed over his lost features. And I didn't know why that
picture came into my head. It was like he knew something
about the night that I didn't. And still don't. I kept swearing at the unconscious body as I dragged it across the
now-wet sand.

35

---◆---

William *was* Sylvia's son. Tony and Sylvia begat William. But Sylvia's mother was a paranoid schizophrenic. To this day. And William was raised as if he would become the same. He did—and became a perfect tool until he began to operate without instructions, on his own. A free demented soul. In fact, both Sylvia and Tony tried to stop him. Sylvia had gotten to him—at the beach out on the pier that day I saw the two lonely figures. Tony and Sylvia were fighting their own wars and had lost control of the only evidence of their love affair. The prophecy of madness had come true. I was certain that William's ending had been ordained at birth.

I had a choice. I could forget the entire affair. I didn't need to explain why William was trying to kill me. He was paranoid. It was easy for the police to believe that he blamed me, sought revenge on me. I could leave Llewelyn alone. Perhaps he would leave me alone. Perhaps he would forget the money. Perhaps he would get religion. Perhaps he didn't want to kill me. Perhaps Julia had suddenly changed his mind. The speculation was wasted. All the perhapses in the world wouldn't permit me to sleep at night. Llewelyn was not a caring, concerned human being at this point. He too had lost control. I knew that the entire parallelogram was going to fall apart. The conspiracy was too ambitious, required too many

players. No game can be played properly with an over
supply of eager, cunning players. All of this I knew in
the consciousness below consciousness. All the time
knew it.

Facing it was a problem. So I got a hotel room for a
couple of days and did something I never do. I drank
In my boozed haze I tried to figure out what was real.
had no luck. Except I knew I would have to deal with
Llewelyn.

Sober, I went to his apartment. I even dressed the part
New suit. Shave, shower. Polished shoes, even cuf
links—opal stones, green-pink-blue eyes at my wrists.

I knocked at the door as if I were a Fuller Brush Man
and stepped aside so he could not see me. I wasn't certain
of what I would say, or do. I was reasonably sure he
would be home. I had lost time. All the burials had taken
place. I knocked again. Waited. Then pounded.

The next door opened. A carbon copy of Pa Kettle
looked up, brow wrinkled, eyes filmed over with nonfat
diluted milk. "I don't see why you have to make all that
noise, mister. It won't wake the dead and it ain't gonna
make him come to the door. No matter what you do."

"I don't understand. Is he gone? What do you mean?"

"I didn't say that now did I? I don't see why a person
can't just take what another person says instead of trying
to make it something else. You a lawyer or something?"

"Excuse me, sir. I just want to know what you know
about your neighbor. He's a good friend of mine. I'm
worried about him."

"Oh, folderol, Sonny. That fellow can take care of him
self." He smacked his lips together as if tasting the las
of a See's chocolate. His ears bent when he spoke, waving
ever so slightly. "You know how big he is?"

"A friend. Remember. He's a friend. Now tell me
where he is. Please."

"Hmm." He thought a moment. Brows furrowed. He

seemed ready to run. "Don't usually tell about neighbors. Not much of a policy. But there's nothin' to tell anyway . . . never is. No secrets anymore, y'know. World's all the same."

"I'm waiting, mister. And I'm beginning to——"

"All right. I didn't say I *wouldn't* tell you. Did I? He hasn't been here. That's what to tell. Nothin'. Just not around. Which I can say is not like him. Once in a while, he doesn't come home!" He had a persistent whine in his voice.

I waved my hand. "Please go inside now, neighbor. I appreciate your help. Just tell me when you last saw him. Or heard him."

"Oh, I *saw* him all right. . . ."

The hall light flickered. He looked up, annoyed, extracted a red cloth from his denims and wiped his eyes. "Damn stupid light. Does that all the time. Can't stand it. Bad eyes anyway. I don't s'pose you know what that's like. You look like a youngster," he cackled, enjoying his trip. "Probably don't know a thing about bad eyes."

"No, I don't," I said, resignedly. "Listen. It's important. When did you last see him?"

"Well, eyes *are* the most important thing. No doubt about it." He looked up quizzically. "Other morning. Lemme see . . ." Eyes with spectacles cast down, measuring my feet. " 'Bout eight in the morning. I was just getting the paper. Oh yeah, that was just yesterday morning. Somehow seems longer," he murmured with his whine. "Just seems like quite a while ago. Y'know how that is?" He drifted off as if time was his only commodity—the past and present mixed together causing quiet reverie.

"And he hasn't been back since?"

He looked up and searched my face. "Everything was quite a while ago, if you know what I mean?"

I didn't have the patience to indulge his regrets. "Now, neighbor, I need to know. He seem OK to you?"

"Seemed so. Do you want me in or out? You told me to go in. Which is it, sonny?" he cackled again, tossing noises from the top of his throat.

He was back in the present. "I want you in. I'm a policeman, too, you see. The captain wants to promote him and we need him down at the Center. So you go on in. I might just wait." I moved toward him slightly, crowding his tight frame backward.

"I'm going, sonny. Don't need to show me how tough you are. Can't see straight anyway. And my wife is sick," he volunteered and then stopped. " 'Course, she's always sick. So that don't count." The cackle began to annoy me. "I'm going. I'm going," waving a manicured hand.

"Thanks. I appreciate your help."

"By the way, Sonny. You are a very dumb cop. Did you know that?"

"How's that?"

A sly light came into his eyes. "You didn't even try the door. It's probably open. He's got nothing to steal, y'know. And he always leaves it open. Says it's easier that way." His eyes squinted. He didn't believe a word I had told him. Calling the police the minute he went inside would be his first order of business.

"I am dumb, neighbor. But I respect other people's doors. The police always respect other people's doors. Didn't you know?"

He rasped another giggle. It wasn't funny. And he disappeared into his apartment.

◆

Lew's living room was scarred. An empty saucer with a half-dozen crumbs of rye toast and a dead glass of milk littered the coffee table. The carton was tipped over onto the floor. The shade on a Kewpie-doll lamp next to the couch tumbled sideways like a sick drunk's hat. Dead magazines hid portions of the sad green carpeting.

I wondered if I had ever really noticed the place before. It had always seemed so nondescript. Like a Holiday Inn family suite twenty miles north of Fresno. An overhead light in the dining room made everything harder and sadder—no soft edges anywhere. I called.

Someone was there. I felt a resignation fall around me. If now was the time, so be it. I didn't want to deal with Llewelyn's hidden plans, his conspiracies, his implied and expressed threats on my existence. I wasn't going to pull any gun, or defend my head or my heart or my anything. At that moment, and very suddenly, I was fearfully vulnerable. It's the same feeling I got when I went berserk at Mary Jarn's. Sometimes that happens, you know, when there's nothing left inside, when nothing seems worth it.

I called again.

"Scared" didn't do my condition justice. Those long arms and legs people told me about felt like silly putty. You learn to make yourself invulnerable and you don't even know you're doing it. Except when someone might blow your torso into an irregular sieve.

The kitchen was empty. A voice on my shoulder hissed, "You're on the last roundup, cowboy." Bullshit. I was no cowboy. No matter. I didn't believe it. "You're on your last roundup, cowboy."

Llewelyn's body caved in the center of his bed. A yellow pillow propped up his head. I wasn't sure at first. "Just couldn't keep away, coudja?" The voice rumbled out of a bare belly covered by chunks of white hair and a .45. His eyes were lidded down to oriental slits. Hands and gun did not threaten. Above the bed a three-masted schooner thrust its weight through boiling seas. An ancient print, brown stains in the sea, tilted as if the entire picture would slide into the menacing water. "Just couldn't do it, could ya? You are one impossible son of a bitch. You act as though it were your manifest destiny to get your fucking head blown off. And believe me," he swept his arm in the direction of the floor "for this kind of money, I intend to do it."

Bundles of money lay in two open briefcases. I couldn't guess how much except it had to be all of Tony's cache plus most of Walter's.

"You got it all, Lew. You certainly did better than a lieutenant's severance check."

"You had your chance . . . you had it. Asshole. You had it. It *is* your destiny to get your head blown off, isn't it?"

His accusation made me stop and get my destiny gears into action. I needed to get the gun off his wide, rolly, hairy belly.

"My destiny is to go on, go on, Lew. Not up, not down, not into some crazy place or good place or infected place—just to go on. On the other hand," I said, reflectively, "your destiny was always never quite making it. That's your story, Mr. Mackin. And it's sad as hell." I sat heavily on a yellow oak chair. "Sad as hell, Llewelyn. Of all the things that might have been." I suspended myself on the fulcrum of the chair, then rested slowly back against the oak bureau. I didn't like oak.

His eyes closed. He was outlined in the pale ceiling light like an Alfred Hitchcock profile. "I have to kill you . . . you son of a bitch who thinks he goes on and on and then some. Oh god, Harvey. You've lost all touch. No one goes on and on unless everything inside is turned off." The eyes flickered. "I've known hundreds like you. They're either pathological killers because there is no feeling left, or drifting old birds, boozed and beaten. Utterly, totally beaten. That's the secret I know about you."

His voice cut into me like iced scalpels. I wanted to run after him, play the child again, beg him not to come after me, disappear like The Shadow, kill him then and there. It had to end then and there . . . somehow. Neither of us could deal with the truth much longer. The damn truth was too much.

"Oh god, yourself, Lew. Goddamn your bilious carcass. Why did you drag me into this? I wanted out at the start dammit!"

Silence. I wanted to turn back time. I wanted to start the summer all over again.

"All the time you were running the show—no, not quite right," I said, remembering. "You and Tony were the Dead End Kids trying to take over. Walter got rich, but so did you. This was a perfect time for your killing, using Henry and Cyril and everyone in sight. And then me. You got me into it. Damn you!"

"Only after Mary ended up at your feet," he protested, sitting up. Ponderously. "I didn't *plan* you into this. You were there! Suddenly you were part of the whole equation as if you had been shot out of a cannon into our laps. There you were. Damn you. In the fucking middle!" His arms rose.

"No. Llewelyn. Let's just stay there. We'll each live a minute or two longer."

He coughed, rolling the phlegm in his throat. "Maybe. Maybe not." Suddenly, like a drug taking hold, gentleness reached out and touched the edges of his eyes. In fact, I thought suddenly that a drug *had* taken over. "A few minutes one way or another is not significant anymore."

"You sound like my high school English teacher," I said. "You know that? Nothing you say sounds like the street. And you and I have been on the street since we were seventeen."

"That's what I am. A frustrated English teacher." He smiled. He sighed. "Confession. My god, Harvey, how one loves to confess. Did you know, Harv, that seventy percent of all murders are not solved by the police? People just confess. They are compelled to confess."

"Why don't you try it?"

He tossed out a half-laugh, wiped his nose. "Much too late."

I said, "Killing me is just another way of suicide for you. Do you see that?"

"I didn't come after you, Harvey."

"You would have."

"Maybe so."

Silence again. He knew what was going on inside me. "I wish I could take it all back," he said. "I wish I could relive every damn minute of the last thirty-five years."

I looked up, realizing that my eyes had been set unseeing, into Lew's pistol. "Forget it, Lew. Blowing a hole into me in your apartment won't make anything go away." For me, it was over, the chord had been played. I didn't *need* his death, didn't want it. He didn't *need* my death. And if he did, I'd have to take my chances.

"I'm leaving," I said, as if pronouncing a sentence. "I'm safe. I didn't know it before. But nothing will happen to me. Not now. And you? You'll probably confess everything about everything. You need to." I rose slowly, stretching. The pistol followed me.

A shroud fell over his face, eyes surrendering to an empty heart. Rage and guilt had gone out of them.

I was free. Llewelyn Mackin couldn't kill me.

The bottom line was that he couldn't kill me. There was no more *kill* left in him.

"Good-bye, Lew. Take the money and run. That's my advice."

As I rose a large hand pressed on my shoulder. A gun barrel touched the back of my head.

"I had to get him out, Harvey," Lew said, "if I wanted the rest of the money. It was all worked out. Tony had it all figured out. I could have money, Julia, and out of this shit cop's existence all at the same time."

Tony smiled distantly. "It's got to look good, Harvey. It's all got to tie in. . . ."

"Except for one little thing, Tony . . . poor William. You didn't figure on me getting him."

"Sorry, chum. All figured. William was lost. No one could help him. I resigned myself to losing him. Sounds bad, huh?"

I could only nod. Llewelyn would not let Tony kill me. I knew it. I absolutely knew it. Tony's eyes gleamed. "We didn't figure you. We figured you to call it quits, to just stay out of it. I would be released from the loony bin and go south forever, and Llewelyn here, well, he would disappear into the sunset with his new wife and all his money, a real winner."

"I suppose you planned to kill Sylvia, too?"

He jabbed the pistol behind my ear, hurting me. "You don't talk about Sylvia. Understand?" Then he relaxed and smiled again. "All I got to do is make it look good . . . tie-in, you know?"

"Go fuck yourself, Tony."

He pulled the pistol back. I could almost hear his finger begin to squeeze. In that second I thought, damn, at least I'm leaving clean. No debts. All paid up. I didn't even feel that I owed Kim anything. You do your best with kids and what turns out, turns out.

The room roared. Llewelyn's gun cracked twice. Anthony Antonnini was thrown into the air like a child's stuffed doll. He lay on the floor twitching away the last of his life, blood splattered about him, trickling from the edges of his eyes.

Mackin's eyes were glazed, lost. "Like I said, Lew. Take the money and run," which I did, leaving blood and insanity behind.

When I was back outside I breathed again. It felt monumentally wonderful.

As I reached to shut the living room door the inevitable self-destructive blast exploded into the room.

I closed the door on everything.

36

———————◆———————

Newspapers carried the story. I got a call from someone at the *Herald* wanting the "inside story." I hung up.

Dutifully, like a mistress, I made entries into my information index. In my journal I wrote:

> The question still remains. On one hand, I'm only an observer. And on the other hand, I'm an ancient moth, drawn to energy, fed by it. I'm between tranquility and turmoil. Mary Jarn was Everywoman— a victim, a toy, a pleasure seeker, a giver of talent and warmth—and weak and strong. Somehow she had touched my soul.

Llewelyn's involvement was never revealed. I was the only key to his secret existence. I told the police almost exactly what happened. I won't tell anybody what happened to the money. But I didn't keep it. There was probably a lot more in some numbered account in the Bahamas. I'd hate to see a transitory strong man on one of those islands confiscate all that blood money. But it's not my affair.

I glanced at the *Racing Form* in my lap. Maybe it had all the answers. Maybe the sea and the *Racing Form* are the only sources of information that a person could have; you can't trust TV or newspapers, or bureaucrats, or good friends, or sons, or wives, or lovers. My mood would change.

At the starting gate the flag was up. Crowd noise grew. Binoculars leapt to noses. Everyone thought their own pari-mutuel ticket was a winner. Some horses were ready and others not quite ready. The park infield was green and peaceful. And the race started.

To the fit, the spoils. To the meek, losing Show tickets.

The entire affair had not hit me yet. A tigerish blue funk would come. In the meantime I was a gambler. A sense of exuberance overcame me. Gamblers believed in winning.

". . . around the far turn———"

My horse was winning. I started chanting, "Stay there baby! Stay there."

". . . now turning into the stretch———"

I was going to win. I knew it. No one was out in the dark aiming at me. Perhaps the world. I didn't care. I wanted them all to be alive. I remembered them. I needed to stop remembering.

"You got that motha fucka, Harvey?"

"You bet I do, Nails! How sweet it is."

For now.